# Humania

By P. J. D.

**RoseDog Books**
PITTSBURGH, PENNSYLVANIA 15238

RoseDog Books
585 Alpha Drive, Suite 103
Pittsburgh, PA 15238
Visit our website at *www.rosedogbookstore.com*

ISBN: 979-8-88812-261-7
eISBN: 979-8-88812-761-2

# Table of Contents:

# 1.
## Pre-plot of an Anti-hero!

A lot of bad shit occurs within this world, and it effects even the whole-heartedness of people. Sad as that fact is, there is nothing coming around or over that fact of life- we are all doomed to travesty of the faintest amount of pressures, a self-reluctant truth.

Something occurred deep within the past that has caused the destruction of that once promising kingdom of Humania, which was the embodiment of peace that this world could possibly create. No wars, no races mattered, no strife, no destruction- only the understanding that people help to contribute towards the rising kingdom and all it stood for. As a result, this place was targeted by invaders- not because of its ideals on peace, but it held the world's largest supply of wealth within its walls. With such, the kingdom created an invincible military in the hopes (as they told the citizens) to protect the peace, but the truth was far darker than anybody could have imagined...

PRESENT TIME:

I have been walking for hours as it seems. I do not know because I lost track of time. Everything happens at once sometimes, and well... I don't know what to say about that. Stupid shit!

I took the road from Annabarde to Calste in the hopes of finding a new place to live for a few days before I moved onto the next stop on my list- death. That's right, I have a death wish. So what? I am too old to care for what other people think, and I certainly do not need younger people telling me to behave and act my age. That is for certain.

The sun is burning bright today, and I am having trouble focusing on my walking. Damn these shoes! I have these old shoes of mine that seem to be two centuries old, but, in reality, they are only a couple of years old, at least. My water supply is running low, so I hope that I arrive to the next town before I run completely out.

TIME PASSES…

I finally see a village far ahead of me that looks like Calste. I feel better at least for making it here before sunset because I hate walking in the dark. Too many memories of the dark. Of the past.

"SHUT UP! SHUT UP!"

Anyway, I entered the town and noticed only a few people out walking around. The people look scared of something. I hate those situations where a town used to be fine and now is full of fear; it only means that a monster or a gang is threatening it, or some form of political corruption. I don't get it, but I guess that I am just an idiot.

I walked towards a stand with an older-looking man, covered in dirt from his head to his feet. He looked as though he just came back from mining. He looked tired, worn-looking, and defeated. I hate the look of defeated people. It always depresses me, and then I can't sleep for another day or so because I run a thousand plans through my head on how to solve that person's problems that are not my own.

"Do you know where I can get some water and food to eat?" I asked the man.

He looked up at me with inward-punctured eyes, and spoke in a soft whisper-like tone that made me lean in to hear him speak:

"There is a building a few buildings down on the right that will have what you are looking for."

"Thanks."

I began walking away and was somewhat confused by something, but I did not know of what yet.

I found the building that the old man was talking about. It read FOOD AND DU… on it. The words had fallen off over the years, I guessed. The building was a regular two-leveled building that was made out of wood and had the distinction of looking well over a century old, when I knew that it was simply at least sixty years old. "Age from the ageless." I once heard long ago by an old friend.

2

Walking into the place, it was a bar-type of setting where there was a bar area, wooden tables, a pianist, a few drunkard men lying around on the floor, and a few rough-looking guys who were playing some cards while drinking. (I always hated people who drank, but that is something for another time).

Walking up to the bar, I asked the barkeep, "Do you have any water to spare a stranger looking for some hydration?"

He looked me over, a crossed-examining glance that I had always received from many strangers before, and I had a feeling that I would always receive for the rest of my life.

"Yeah. Over there in the corner. Just take what you want and pay me for what you got."

I nodded my head and went over to fill up my canteen.

As I did so, however, I heard a scream from upstairs. I looked around and saw that nobody else was looking, nor caring about, the direction in which the voice came from. I silently filled up my canteen, and right before I went to leave, I heard another scream and what sounded like a cry for help from a feminine voice. I went to walk up the stairs, but I was overtaken by some men who had grabbed me and told me to stay out of whatever business was going on upstairs.

"I heard somebody crying up there." I told them.

One of the men who grabbed me looked familiar, and he grinned with all yellow-colored teeth. He licked his lips, and said in a deep voice:

"That's none of your business. We do things the way we like here, and no outsider is coming in here to stop that. So, I guess that you should go finish what you need to do and leave this place."

"Before I leave, I want to ask you something."

"What is it?"

"Is your name 'Thompson the Crack'?"

"If it is, then want business it is of yours?"

"Nothing, I just want to tell you that you won't make it out of this building alive, that is all." I said as I began to laugh.

All the other guys began to laugh at me before Thompson spoke again.

"You want to die now? I have nothing better to do today. Take him out will ya boys?"

I was surrounded in a moment by five men who had guns, swords, and their bare hands as weapons. I hate my luck when it comes to places like this. Why can't they ever come easily?

One guy came at me, and I grabbed the sword in his hand and broke it into many pieces. Then, I placed my hand on his face before I slammed his whole body down towards the floor where he went straight through into the cellar below.

Another two guys came at me with their bare hands, and I grabbed one of them before they could hit me, and promptly broke his arm before swinging him around in the air (by his broken arm. I felt it coming out of its socket), and through him into the other guy as hard as I could. Let's just say that they won't be moving ever again.

The last two guys fired a few shots at me that made contact. I grunted in slight pain before I charged at one of them, punching them straight in the chest, breaking their ribs, and crushing their heart in the process. All of this blood mess could have been avoided if they only let me go upstairs.

After such, I quickly grabbed the other man and tossed him over the bar where he was impaled by the broken glasses that he landed on.

Looking at Thompson the Crack, I smiled before I spoke to him:

"Now, it's your turn, Crack."

"Don't come near me!" He fired a shot at me that did nothing but go straight through me.

"Who are you?" He asked.

"I'm here to kill you piece of shit for what you did seven years ago."

"Seven years ago? That means…Wait, you were in Binstool weren't you? You can't be that man that chased up out of town! I though we killed you back then." He trembled in fear.

"Well. I'm here now, and quite alive. I'm here to kill your sorry ass for no other reason but because I set my eyes on your butt, and when I set my eyes on a victim, then they don't have a chance in Hell to live."

He tried to run, but I grabbed him, and punched at his face, breaking his jaw in the process. I took his arms and broke them too- just for the humiliation of it. I even took out one of his eyes. After that, I looked at him one final time before throwing him through the wooden wall, and well through the next four buildings down the road.

I smiled and licked the blood from my hands. I licked some more off the walls and floors until I felt more hydrated. I laughed a little before I decided to take my water and some food from what was left of the bar area. Nothing beats beating the shit out of a person before helping some poor soul out of whatever situation that they found themselves in.

Walking over to the stairs, I began to climb them on my way towards where I heard the scream, and help the poor, sad idiot who was in trouble. Life sucks sometimes, but what can you do?

Fin.

To be continued in part II.

# 2.
## *Anti-Hero Part 11*

The city of Humania became a great nation of great military strength, and the once held kingdom of peace and serene atmosphere became a warzone. People started working towards creating weapons to protect against invaders. The walls of the city were armed with archers, machine guns, and catapults, while the inner city was guarded by heavy armed soldiers who were trained by the aspiring General, Toadas Piker- a man who came from a wealthy family, and a long line of abusive men who sailed through the ranks by the means of his own strength instead of his families' fortune. Men strolled the city walls by the hours, all looking the same in their uniforms- a dark grey outfit with pockets in every place that you could think of.

It came as no surprise that the once peace-driven kingdom changed in some respects, but as whole, the kingdom remained with its original ideals set forth. A place built from every culture and none at the same time. A place that welcomed people from everywhere, of every faith, of every sex, of every understanding, and of every language. Nothing was off-limits for the kingdom, except for the rules that the city created for its citizens to follow. For as we all know, a kingdom without rules is liable to fall to pieces over no order. However, that is just another part of the story...

PRESENT:

I walked up the stairs to try and find that person who screamed so damn loudly to wake the dead. As I looked down the hallway, I noticed all the doors were locked except for one single one. Of course, it would be that door. I am tired of rescuing people who are always in an open door. Nobody knows how to make things tough for an idiot anymore. Damn idiots!

I walked down the hall to that door, and I looked within the crack of the door to see inside. I could only make out red all over the side of the wall. When I opened that door, I took a deep breath in as I glanced at the scene before me.

The person who screamed was a woman. She was alive then, but when I was dealing with those shitheads downstairs, the person who had her in here had killed her. I wished that I would have pushed those guys out of the way, but when people begin to tell me what to do, I get real pissed and decide to lose my temper, and well…you know what happened.

She laid motionless on the bed with no clothes on. Her neck looked snapped off, and her insides were gutted open with a knife. The animal could not even bother to place a blanket on her before they escaped. Her eyes were still opened. I closed them out of decency for her memory. Poor fool.

The window was open. I glanced out and saw a few people walking around, some the same and others a few new who had obviously just woken up or something.

I just sighed and went out of the room and headed downstairs. There was nobody left in the building after what occurred, so I decided to leave this building. I walked outside. The sun had gotten hotter since I arrived here. I hate the heat, it only slows me down, but I'm used to it by now.

Anyway, I went into the street and went up to a man who was half-sleeping on the side of the building. I could smell him from here; he wore torn clothes that gave a clear impression of his situation in life, but that wasn't for me to judge. I walked up to him and whispered in his ear:

"Hey, where is the undertaker?"

He slowly opened his eyes and stared at me before speaking. "I see him in front of me."

I sighed. "No, you idiot! I mean, where is the undertaker for this poor town?"

He glanced at me. "He is working right now. Burying old 'One-eyed Mike' up yonder hill over there."

He pointed a weak finger up to a short hill where I saw a man that wore all black and had a shovel in his hand.

"Thanks." I said before leaving him to his life.

## TIME PASSES

I was nearing the undertaker and he looked young. His face had no hair on it, but his face was worn-looking from years of being in this hot sun. I didn't want to talk to him, but I had to tell him about the bodies.

"Are you this poor town's undertaker?" I asked.

He stopped shoveling dirt and thought for a minute before answering me (without even turning around to face me).

"Yeah. I am him."

"Well, there is about six bodies at the bar in town."

"Did you put some of them there?" He asked me in a deep, sorrow-filled tone. As if he were my parent.

"For your information, I put five of them there, but the last one is a female who looks like she was raped, tortured, and gutted to death." I said to him.

He seemed moved by what I said because he faced me, and said, "I will come by in a few minutes to pick them up." He barely had any life left in those dark brown eyes of his. "Will you mind telling me who all is dead? If you know any of their names, that is?"

"One of them was called 'Thompson the Crack', and the other five I don't know their names, nor do I care." I told him.

"How bad is the place?" He asked me out of nowhere.

"If you're talking about this place, it's a shithole, but I have seen worse. As for the bar that I was at, I think that I made a few improvements. A few tables broken, the bar smashed up, and a leftover surprise to get people talking."

He sighed again before speaking to me. "This town never was this bad before. It was peaceful years ago. People came here to trade, to eat, and to rest, but then the whole incident in Humania caused a downturn in this place. Many towns and places far away benefitted from the kingdom. We believed that we all had a chance to live and be as we all wanted to be. A place where people worked to help the whole of the kingdom inspired many people that I once knew that they could make a change and bring peace to the larger world and live by the example that the kingdom set for its people. Things have been different for decades now since the fall, and…"

I stopped him in his tracks. "Look, I don't care about this place. I came here for food and water. Instead, I have a few bullets, blood, and a few dead people. Your problems are your concern. Leave me out of them! I just came to tell you about those dead people before leaving." I told him in an angered mood.

He looked down at the ground, and before I turned away from him, he said, "I understand. You have your problems to deal with. Take some water from the side of the church. Thank you, for telling me about the bodies. I'll take care of them."

With that, I left. I was sick of this stupid place. Everywhere I go, it's the same sob story. "We were better off when the kingdom was around... We felt that we all had a chance for peace..." What a tone of shit!

I took his advice and grabbed some water for me to take with me. I didn't care to eat anything because I wanted to leave this place as soon as possible. It was leaving a poor taste in my mouth.

That is how things were for me. Walking from place to place, hearing sob story after sob story, and killing a few assholes who deserved it. I can't stand this life for long, but I have always been afraid to take that leap and end it all. My parents were caring people, and they raised me better than just taking my whole life. It is their fault that I can't die by myself.

"Stop thinking! Stop thinking!"

MOVING FORWARD

I was walking out of this town, now. Finally, I can move on and find the next "great town" for me to hear stories, kill people, and receive useless advice. I can't stand life sometimes. Yet, I find some days more enjoyable than others. After walking, I can just sit down and sleep for hours if I wanted and nobody can tell me what to do, and if they do, then they can visit a hot place awaiting them.

When I began walking, I silenced out my thoughts and just simply looked at the sky. The sun. The blue sky. The birds. The clouds. The emptiness... and there it is. This, the point where I begin to feel self-hatred for myself. Day after fricking day, I do this. Life is boring without change, and I hated this point for the last twenty-eight years.

TIME SKIP BECAUSE WHY NOT

A few hours after walking, I saw something in the distance. Another thing to deal with! Why can't the universe leave me alone and deal with everybody else for once? I know plenty of people that it could help while it wastes its time with me. Anyway, as I kept getting closer to whatever thing was in front of me, I noticed it wasn't moving.

Of course, it wasn't moving! Maybe, it is a building, a dead animal, or something else not worth my time.

Once I was within feet of whatever this thing was, I saw that it was a broken-down stagecoach. What are we in the Old West? Who the Hell came up with this setting for my luck? This is why people suck! They don't have any imagination left for themselves to spare for people like me or you.

Glancing at this stagecoach, however, I saw that is looked older than a decade. The wheels were gone (probably because somebody stole them for money or something), and the glass was gone. Yet, when I looked at where the glass used to be, a cloth was covering its place from the inside, so as to keep the forces of nature out. I wonder if somebody used to live here.

I slowly approached the coach, and as I neared, I heard a noise from within the coach. After not hearing it again, I came closer to the door. I opened it, and I looked around. The coach was full of stuff ranging from wood to metal, from clothes to liquids in jars, and other stuff that looked like junk to me. However, I looked in the nearest corner of the coach, and I saw a little person in the corner.

Great! A person who may need help. Well, I guess that I should ask if they need something.

"Hey, do you need help?" I asked in as nice voice that I could tolerate.

The figure hesitated, I guessed, but after a few seconds, they came out and I could see them clearly. It was a little girl, possibly seven or ten (I could not tell either way). She was rather small. An orphan! Well, there goes my time.

"Are you lost? Where are your parents?"

She looked at me a little scared. I went down on both of my knees to make her feel less intimidated. She came closer to me, and this time reached out her hand to touch my arm. She squeezed it. Looking at my clothes, and at my face for some reason. Finally, she let go of my arm and looked at my eyes- almost studying my mind, my soul.

"I don't know. Could you help me find them?" She asked in a low whisper.

"Why did they leave you here?" I asked.

"My father sent me here to find my mother, but when I was arriving, we were attacked."

She stopped talking. She just trembled in place. I saw a tear come from her eyes.

I felt uncomfortable, but I had to do something to get this kid to stop crying, so I reached out and placed my hand on her head before she opened her eyes in shock.

She looked at me, then at my hand. The next thing I knew, she rushed into my body and held onto me. I wanted to pull her off. To tell her to get lost, but I felt her trembling.

"Can you help me?" She asked while crying into my chest.

I looked at her, then at the coach, and again back to her. I was going to hate myself even more for this later, but…

"Sure." I spoke.

She kept holding me tightly, and I passed the time away in my head kicking myself for getting involved in something that was, yet again, not my problem. Anyway, I decided to let my mind drop off there and just face that I was helping this kid for who knows how long.

"Is this a good idea?" I asked myself.

Fin.

To be Continued in the next story.

# 3.
## Teared-up Reproach

She kept holding onto me, and it was annoying as time passed on. She would not stop crying into my chest as I had my arms around her. Sheesh! This is dragging on too long.

I looked down at her and could see her shaking a little, but I just kept staring at her. Who the Hell would send a child out here to find her own mother without an escort or something? This is just one reason that I find people all spinless pieces of shit and filth. They can't get their own priorities straight, and it pisses me off!

"Motherfucker! I have to say something." I thought.

Looking at her, I asked. "Do you know who your mother is? What she looks like?"

She sniffled and spoke in a soft tone. "No. I don't know her name. I don't even know what she looks like. My father just packed me up here and told me that my mother is waiting for me." She then began to cry again.

I hate how children can cry so much.

So, her ass of a father sent her out here to find her mother that she does not know of, or what she looks like. Yeah, the bastard sent her away because he was sick of her. Piece of shit! When I tell people something, I don't hold back. "I want you gone because you are a no-good, cunt-marked of a child, so get out of here." Yet, he had to make up a lie, that bastard.

"Well, what do you want me to do for you?" I asked her in as un-angered of a tone that I could make myself use.

She looked up at me, and I could see her red, tear-stained eyes that still held a shine in them. Even as she still looked at me with a scrunched-up face from her tears- her cheeks close to her eyes, her eyes half-closed, and her mouth opened wide in the way that people cry in.

"What?" She asked confused.

"Do you want me to help you find her?"

She looked deep in thought for a moment before saying, "No... I want to leave this place. I don't like this place anymore."

Smart kid. She could at least make a decision like that at her age- that's a good thing.

"Okay. What do you want to do, then?"

"I want to go home."

God, she is a bigger idiot than I thought. I sighed and just looked at her for a moment before I spoke:

"Fine. Where do you live? I can try to get you home."

"I live in Yondaster."

"WHAT?????????????????????????"

I closed my eyes and breathed. There is no way that this kid came from Yondaster. That place in a five months' worth of a journey on a good day. If you hit any storms, any beasts, any thieves, or anything else, it would take almost a whole year to make it back to that place. I hate long journeys.

"GOD WHY ME?"

TIME PASS

I had gotten the kid to collect her things that she had with her, and we set out on foot to her homeland of Yondaster. Sometimes, I think that I am being punished for all the shit that I had done in life. Every fricking time that I traveled to a place, I would always end up helping somebody. I blame many people for this quality, but mainly I blame my parents (but that's a whole other thing that I could care less to talk about).

We had been walking now for a good three hours. Our progress was hindered because this kid was so weak, and so unused to doing strenuous activities, that she would need to take breaks. After it happened for the fifth time, I stopped, turned around, and faced her while on my knees.

"Are you hungry?" I simply asked her.

She nodded, and I handed her an apple that I was saving for myself.

"Here take this. You have to keep your strength up, or you will be too weak to even make it back to your home."

She took the apple and began to eat it like a ravenous animal that hasn't eaten anything for two days. As she was eating the apple, I could see her taking glances at me from the corner of my eyes. Why the Hell am I helping this kid? Is there something that I am missing here, or am I truly the weak one here?

"Thank you." She said when she finished the apple.

I nodded and we continued onward. The next town would not be in sight for another three days according to my memory. As the evening passed, the sun beamed down on as with its last rays of heat, slowly sinking over the mountain tops that lined the passages far away from us. I never felt entirely comfortable with the sun during the day. I like the night. It gives me a sense of security that the sun doesn't. Exposed or composed? What do other people prefer? I hate when I get thoughts like these in my head because it only depresses me. Thinking about other people only fills me with pear hatred because people to me are just pathetic pieces of meat that deserve whatever comes their way (I only pity the ones that don't pity themselves, which is less than I always see in the human race).

As evening came, I stopped and looked around. I noticed a large boulder off to the side of our path that looked good enough for a semi-secure campsite.

"We are stopping for tonight to make camp."

I pointed to the boulder, and she followed me over. When we walked around it, I saw that the boulder had another over hanging, but slightly smaller, boulder on top of the first that acted as a little shelter from the rain.

We sat down on the ground, and I set down my bag that I had around my shoulders. I told her to stay with my bag, and that I would go and grab some firewood.

Once, I grabbed some firewood, I set up the fire, and lighted it. My survival skills are only as good as when they are used for other people. That is another curse of mine.

As the fire burned, I looked over at the girl who was shivering in the night's cold air. I took off my heavy jacket and placed it around her as a blanket to keep her warm.

"Thank you." She spoke up to me.

"Don't worry about it." I said to her.

We just stared at the fire for a long time. However, I could not help but wonder what my life would be for the next year. This girl had something about her that seemed special. Maybe a secret power? Wealth? Perhaps, she possessed information that was crucial to somebody? Still, I could not shake the feeling that she held something deeper to her than she was showing me.

Suddenly, I realized that I don't even know her name. "Idiot! Taking in a stray without getting her tag number or name." I thought to myself. Man, I have been thinking to myself a lot lately. I hate that.

"Hey, what is your name?"

She looked at me, and she said, "It is Claire."

Well, I now have a name to who I am helping.

"What is your name?" She asked me.

"It is Eilif." I told her.

"Hello, Eilif." She said while smiling.

I grinned and laughed. It has been years since I had company with me. It felt somewhat nice, but I knew deep down that it would end. Time never lasts forever.

We didn't say anything else after that. I don't know what's going through her head. Adults are easy to read. They are all jokes. They are all so pathetic and useless that I can read their mind so easily. However, when it comes to children, I can't ever tell what they are thinking of. I guess it is the distinction between time and life experiences. The idea that you should stay young and enjoy life before you become heartless. Whoever said that I would like to cut off one of their limps because that is the same advice that people have been giving me since I was little, and it always pissed me off when people said it. My temper is one thing, but that phrase is a death sentence for whoever says it. Yet, I just did. Shit! I hate my life sometimes.

The fire started to die down, and so, I through some more wood in it, and I laid against the giant boulder so that I could lean against something while I slept. As I closed my eyes, I felt something lay next to me, and bundle up close to me. I opened one of my eyes and saw that it was Claire who eased her way next to me and covered herself with my jacket.

"What are you doing?" I asked her.

"I have trouble sleeping by myself in strange places, and I'm scared."

I looked at her eye and noticed a few tears coming down onto her cheek. I wiped them away, and I told her in a tired tone:

"Bundle up. It gets cold at night."

I saw her smile. I stayed up for a while longer to look at the fire. It burned just as the kingdom did. The people. The homes. The ideas. The souls. Everything burned. I hated myself for remembering that place because it meant nothing to me anymore, but I guess your memories never die (especially, when you have someone that keeps reminding you of those memories).

Time passes and the pain remains, and I hate that. My mother used to say something about how time is a wonderful experience, but she was a lost women who lost what sense she had long before the destruction of life occurred.

"Whatever is next, it's my move to make." I thought to myself.

Fin.

# 4.
## To Know is to Begin Again Part 1

I awoke to the blinding light of the morning. My eyes slowly adjusted to the brightness before I could see.

"Damn! Morning already. I want to kill myself sometimes." I thought in my mind.

I looked down and noticed that Claire was still sleeping on me. Annoying! Yet, I could not bear to wake her up. I knew than most the destruction that a lack of sleep can cause a person, but for me, it grew easier over time through my training and journey around this decerped planet that we live upon.

I gently moved Claire off me and sat her head on the ground. When I got up, I went to the remains of last night's fire. It still retained the heat from the last remaining strands of charcoal that now laid within the pile. I went towards the pile of wood that I had gathered and returned to the fire. I placed the wood into the fire with the hopes of restoring a large enough flame to eat some morning grub.

As I was searching for food, I glanced at the girl before me. Now that I look at her, I can notice the little details that escaped me when I first found her. Her hair was dark brown with strays of dirt within it, her hands were rather small for a girl her age, which I estimated at around twelve or younger perhaps, and her body was rather slim and weak looking. The look on her face showed that she had not slept in a long time. I always recognize that look. That look of peace that a person gets when you finally sleep for a whole night- and it was pleasant. I wish that I had those, but my dreams…never mind. They don't matter anymore.

Anyway, as I placed my pot above the fire with my bacon and beans in it, Claire slowly rose from her slumber and looked around until she saw me. At first, she looked scared. Like she saw a ghost, but that look went away. I know that look all too well to. What is wrong with this world? I hate when a person can't sleep one fucking night without a bitch of a dream coming in and screwing with your head. Those damn dream pigs!

"How are you today? Did you sleep well?" I asked the girl.

She looked at me with a tired look. "Yeah," she began," I slept great. Where are we?"

"We are around a mile or so from the last town that I picked you up at. We are a three-day journey to the next town. Want something to eat?"

"Yes!" she yelled excitably.

I handed her a plate of bacon and beans to eat. Before I started eating my portion, I saw that she gulfed down her meal in two bites.

"Shit man! She must have been starving." I thought as I stared at her.

After she finished her meal, she handed me her plate. I ate mine slowly. Nothing more was said for the next few minutes, and I honestly enjoyed the quietness. However, when I finished my food and I began to clean up the plates, the girl looked at me with an intense stare. One of those stares that a child gives to something that they want or find interesting. Which one it was for me, I do not know, nor do I care. People's opinions of other people die off pretty quickly when you realize that opinions are fabricated from the very culture that put them in your heads. The society has nothing to do with them, nor does the stories that you read or listen to. A person's opinions are founded and set up brick by fucking brick, and cemented in with cunt-paste, into place in a person's mind through the culture that a government creates for its citizens.

"NO, I'M NOT COMPLAINGING!!!" I screamed to myself. It has been years since I came to this conclusion, and it depresses me quickly. So, I will end this here!

"Who are you?" I heard somebody ask, which brought me out of my inner conversation with myself. Thank you, God, for the distraction.

"I am Eilif. A simple man who is on a journey." I stopped myself there in the hopes that this would be enough to quench her thirst for prying information out of me.

"Where are you going?" she asked me.

"Damn this kid! I want to already bang my head against this rock. Why did I help her again?" I asked myself in my head. The decisions that I make. Isn't life just great?

"Nowhere in particular. I am just trying to leave behind some memories that I don't want to remember."

"Oh." That is all she said before looking into the fire. I felt bad for her, but she is just another senseless victim of the world that could not suck on the nectar coming from the breast of the Earth's all-forgiving grace. Fuck you, Earth! The extremes to live or to die mean little to this environment that everybody is in. Since the Fall, the world has never been the same. Plagues. Wars. Famine. Revolutions. Meteor strikes. Volcanic eruptions. The ice melting. Lastly, the lands all colliding into each other to form this new world that we all inhabit.

LATER ON, THE DIRT ROAD

We had been walking for who knows how long. The sun slowly rose-up into the sky before halting in place to keep its ever-beaming heat upon us. I was used to it, though (that doesn't mean that I like the sun. I still hate it).

As we walked, we passed along a dirt road in an open setting until that gave way to a half forest and half hill location. We walked along the edge of the hill. I looked down and thought about all the poor suckers who have fallen down it, or about all those who have lived after the fall. They could have died, and it would not have mattered.

After finally making our way around the hillside with a cliff drop, I decided to stop for Claire's sake. She had been falling behind me now for the last hour.

"We are going to stop here for now and pick up in twenty minutes." I said as I laid my bag down on the ground adjacent to the road that we were just traveling on.

"Okay." She said before almost falling down onto the ground onto her butt.

TIME PASS

The break did not help because Claire only seemed more tired than before. God, I hated people like that! You know those fat-assed people, or stick-people, who can't travel more than a few miles before falling to pieces. It makes me angry. Fucking weaklings, but I have no excuse to complain.

As the sun slowly drew down, I glanced around me and felt that we were being watched almost, but I don't know if it is because I am paranoid or not.

"I don't need this right now." I thought to myself. If some random thieves were going to take anything we have on us, then they could at least grow some balls and just come on out already.

Time passed shortly, and I waited for anymore faint sounds, but I heard nothing. I hate this so much. Shit!

Claire suddenly stopped walking, and as I looked at her, I saw fear on her face. She was terrified beyond belief.

"What is it now?" I asked somewhat annoyed. Before I knew it, though, I got hit in the back on the head by a hard, blunt weapon, and I went unconscious.

DAKNESS.      DARKNESS.      Darkness.      DARK-NESS!!!!!!!!!!!!!!!!!!!!!!!!!!!!!!!!!!!!!

*"Wake up." I heard that voice say.*

*"Wake up you animal."*

*"You are the animal here, not me." I said to IT.*

*"Right. You forget that I know you both inside and out. Rise. The time has come to Rise."*

*I felt myself losing grips with my sense.*

*"No, not again. You aren't coming out." I took a few breathes and tried to focus my mind on the matter on hand. "This is my body. This is my body. This is my life." I repeated.*

*"You need me, now." It said once again.*

*"No, I don't. Leave me alone."*

*"Well, if you ever want to save the offspring, then you should wake up soon." The voice finally said before leaving my senses completely.*

*"WAIT? What?"*

OUT OF THE DARKNESS

I awoke. My head hurt, but besides that I felt fine. I looked around and noticed that my bag was still here, but something was missing. "Shit! What truck hit me?"

Wait! Where is Claire? I looked and could not see her anywhere. Shit! Motherfucker! Pissed-assed pig of complete feces! She is gone. I let my guard down for one damn second, and now she is gone.

I gritted my teeth. So, there was someone watching us. I was right, and now they have the kid that I promised to return to her family. I am a complete waste of a human.

I stood up, and as I regained more of myself, I thought of what to do. If they are bandits, it does not matter if they have a camp in the woods or a cave. If they jumped us, then they obviously needed supplies or money to buy more supplies. There is only once place that is close enough to here that they can trade other people's supplies to buy supplies, and that is the human-disposal, sheer-undignified town of Bonterkide.

"Well. I guess that I have to rescue this brat. If I make it out of this alive, I swear that I will kill someone for this."

I began walking to Bonterkide.

Fin.

To be continued next.

# 5.
## *To Know is to Begin Again Part II*

"It had to be Bonterkide that she would be taken to. Shit!" I thought to myself as I was walking. "Of course, they had to take her to that abyss of human-Hell."

I already knew that we had to travel that way in the first place, but we were going to be there for a short time. What they do to people there is beyond inhuman. Replacing peoples' body parts with robotics parts from old, rusted machines that no longer work. Replacing peoples' parts with sliced and torn-up animal parts that still leak blood. Infection. Prostitution. Making people fight for a key to their salvation, and that salvation is the prospect of going outside for ten minutes. They keep their captives in cages and keep them in low-down bunkers or abandoned warehouses. That is not even the worst part. If anybody ever gets pregnant, I heard, they take that person and forcibly slice them open, rip out both eggs, douse them in gasoline, and burn them in front of that gutted person. Again, there is worse things about this place, but I can't stomach it sometimes.

I regret taking the kid this way. The bandits around this area are known for killing families and taking the children for multiple activities: torture, sexual humiliation, breeding, fighting, bait for other people, and sometimes if the food supply is low, they sell them for food (but, if no one takes them, then they are eaten alive). Man, this placed is fucked-up, but I don't care either way. I don't live here. I don't have the right to tell people how to live. There are no rules, no law, no connections, no hope, no peace- it is all about who you want to be to survive. Either you stay in town or risk a three-to-five-day journey to the next town with no supplies. Can you blame people for staying, then?

Anyway, I have been walking all day. The night has slowly come upon me; however, I did not stop to rest. I don't know what is so special about this girl that makes me want to help her so. I never wanted to help anybody else but myself before. So, why do I now feel a need to help her? Does it all come back to my helpful nature? Shit! Why can't I ever change that part about myself?

"Do I need to change myself, or do I need to change my mind?" I thought to myself.

I don't like being introverted in this way. Once, I get lost in my thoughts, "It" wants to come out and play, but I can't have that. If that thing wants to come out, then everybody else will, and I do not need that now.

Stay focused. Stay clear. Stay in the moment.

MORE TIME PASSES ONWARD

I had walked through the night and into the early morning. The sun showed itself with all of its brightness. The wind had died down, and now all that remained was a faint coolness within the air.

I don't remember quite how long that I have to until I arrive to Bonterkide, but it should be within the evening, I suppose.

The more that I walk, the more aching my body feels. I am used to walking a long distance, but not without a least a small break. I'm not young, anymore. Damn, why do I have to say that to myself? Well, I always thought of myself as old in the first place, but that was a joke. This is what happens to people. As they age, they tell themselves that they are only as old, or as high-spirited, as they want to be, but the truth is that we all grow old. Our bodies slow down. Our muscles weaken. Our thoughts die off. Our minds go, and worst of all, we can't do a damn thing about it. We watch as puppets attached to the string of time. That is what that string is- the damn string of time that holds us in place, keeping our souls in place, and lusting after our precious time until we wither away. Never let anybody tell you that you are worth time, when the actual truth is that nobody is worth time. Not you! Not me! Not anybody within this shit-pieced together world that we live upon!

However, that is something only an idiot would think about, and as I said before, I'm an idiot.

I continued walking. I kept my mind clear the rest of the way- only straying away here and there when I noticed a bird fly by me. That reminds me about when I was young... No! No! No! Stop it! No thinking anymore. I'm sick of this PMSing-trash!

ONCE ON THE VERGE

I finally made it to this shithole. It took every effort not to fall and just sit outside the town for a few minutes. Instead, I breathed in the rotten-flesh flavored air that had a hint of oil, piss, onions, and tar within the back-burning essence of the air. I never enjoyed this place.

I started walking into the town. The one good thing about this place is that people are so pre-occupied with their own issues that they don't look at me. I don't get stares within this town. That's good. I hate people looking at me. Thinking about what my business is, and why am I walking that way instead of this way. Questioning glances, that is what I hate most of all, but this place does not have that. People tend to their own shit, and they leave mine out of theirs.

Except now. I have to find where that trading building is. If I remember correctly, I think it was down Stant Street. I walked off in that direction.

This place hasn't changed at all. The windows are broken through. Blood lines the street. Shit covers all the front porches of homes. I saw a person fucking a corpse in the middle of the street.

"Yep. Nothing has changed here, that's for sure."

I kept walking down this street. The main thing to remember is that you should never look anybody in the eyes. That brings trouble, and I don't want to deal with anybody else while I'm here rescuing Claire.

For the most part, this place remained that same, yet I felt that there was something different here. I felt an almost oppressed feeling that is shadowing the people of this place. Someone has obviously scared these people into paying for something, or threatening them for money, which no one has. Some dumb, retarded person frozen in the time of money equals power, and that the only way to get that money and power is to invoke fear. Don't they know that such an idea is over-used? Dumb shits!

Anyway, that aside, I arrived at the building that I was looking for. "FRONKS & SIDE-OBJECTS", that is what it read. It has been years since I was last here.

"Well, here goes nothing." I though as I walked into the store.

It remained the same over the years, at least. The store looked like an old drug store from back in the past, but instead of what you might expect on the shelves, there was only body parts. They kept the good stuff in the Trunk Room.

I walked up to the register where a woman stood. She had blond hair, a rough-looking face with some wrinkles, a robotic, thin arm on the right side of her body, and she was smoking a cigar. An image of female-emasculation.

"Well, look who came in here." She said as she noticed me.

"Hey, Roan. How have things been?" I asked her.

"Not too much since the last time you were here. Except that we had to rebuild the storage house that you destroyed a while back."

"I already apologized about that, and it wasn't really my fault." I sighed.

"Well, anyway. What do you want? Are looking for another good time?" she asked me.

"No. I'm here to find someone. Have you heard about any bandits coming into town either today or yesterday?" I looked away from her.

She thought for a moment. "Yeah, some bandits arrived in town this morning with a little girl. Cute, too. Why do you want to know?" she gave me a questioning look.

"I promised to bring her home." I flatly said.

"Whoa! Who would have thought big, destructive "Demon of the Hell Core" would be helping a child." She started laughing at my expense.

I walked up to her and gave her a death stare. She always tries my patience. "This bitch." I thought.

"Yeah, I found her on the side of the road starving to death, and for your damn information, I don't like to be laughed at. You may know what you know through your sources, but I swear to my ever-growing anger that if you don't tell me where they are having their meeting, I will destroy this whole town. You may think you know everything about me, but you have no fucking idea! Now could you please tell me what I need to know, Roan?" I yelled at her, though the last part of what I said was softer.

She looked at me with a bewildered look. "You never said 'please' to me for anything before. This kid is really rubbing off on you. Finally, some manners." She chuckled somewhat.

Before I could yell again, she pressed a button under the counter and a door opened-up where a shelf rested against the wall. "Follow that tunnel for about a half mile, and you will be at the warehouse. Try not to destroy it, please."

I nodded at her and walked through the entryway. It was slightly dark, but there where lanterns that brightened the tunnel for me. "That damn woman. Who the Hell does she think that she is? Laughing at me for helping somebody. Fuck you, Roan!" I screamed in the tunnel knowing that she would be listening via the audio sound system that she made me install years ago.

PASSING TIME

I found my way through the tunnel. It led out to a cave exit that led to a clearing of grass. There were mountain tops surrounding us on all time. The surrounding land was covered in grass, and while staring upwards, I noticed that there were cliffs all around this area (almost so that it resembled a bowl shape of a valley).

I walked onto the grass and kept walking. Eventually, I saw a warehouse in the distance that was rather large in nature. Broken down trucks laid all around. Unfinished structures of what would be buildings were covered in vines. Life was barren looking. It was an old construction site left to rot for the ages to come.

Walking up to the building, it looked torn up. Gunshot holes. Parts of the building that rotted away. Bomb craters on walls of the place. I don't like this place. It reminds me too much of what awaited me. The pain of remembering what I left behind for this new life.

Carefully, I opened the door so that I would not make a sound. However, the door creaked anyway because of how damn old it is. I looked inside and it was all dark. Of course, this was not going to be easy, and because of how big this place is, it will take me some time to find their hiding hole. I walked in and simply walked around everywhere trying to find any sign of life. I smelled something in the air:

"Smells like blood." I thought.

I took no time in going towards the back end of the building where I saw a large metal door, and a large man standing in front of it. Why does nobody ever think that placing a person in front of a door makes it more questioning? Stupid people. They were much better at these things years ago. Thieves had brains back then, at least.

After glancing at the man, I saw all his tattoos, his bulging muscles, and his incredible height. Like I care. He is another pushover. Why can't people challenge me anymore? I swear!

I walked up to him. He looked at me in a confused way. Finally, after looking me up and down he spoke:

"What do you want?"

"I want to get into the sale." I flatly put it.

He looked at me again. "What is the password?" Damn this is how bandits do things! Passwords? Fuck this guy's passwords!

"I don't know it." I told him.

"Then you can't come in. Get lost." He told me.

I sighed. So, this is how it's going to be then?

"Fine. I tried asking nicely, but you forced my hand."

He reached down for me, but before he touched me, I grabbed his hand and crushed it down to the bone, breaking it, and dislocating his wrist from his arm. After that, he tried to kick me, but I grabbed it, and swiping my leg, I managed to make him come crashing down onto the ground. Once he was on the ground, I proceeded to break both of his legs by ripping them out of his torso. All the meanwhile, I heard him scream as tears shed down his cheeks. Think about that. A grown man crying. Now that is funny.

I leaned down to his face, and I said into his ear:

"Now, can I come in?"

He nodded his head, and as he handed me the key to open the door, I grabbed his large body and threw it at the door, breaking it down, and tossing the door a good five feet away. I walked inside, and I saw a bunch of men looking at where their doorman laid on the ground, bleeding out, and unconscious. They then looked at me in a questioning look. I walked in.

"Hello. I decided to let myself in." I said to them.

They looked at the battered man before them, and I saw one man throw up in the corner upon what he was looking at. "Wimp." I thought.

"What do you want?" one of the men asked.

"I am looking for a little girl that was with me that you poor bastards took after knocking me out." I said to them.

They looked at each other, and a man came out of a back-room area who looked to be the main guy in charge.

"If you want her, then you have to pay up." The dork said.

"I'm not paying for a girl that was taken from somebody else."

"Then, you don't get her. Boys show him out."

Three guys walked up to me, but I delivered a swift kick to one of the men's chests while grabbing a man with my left arm and flipping him into the ground. Once they were done, the other man charged at me before I cut a hand upwards to his jaw, forcing it to pop, and then delivering a straight hit to his right peck, which sent him flying. In total, one man's body was currently in a wall, the other was in a crater in the ground, and the third flew into a few crates, breaking at least six.

The men looked at me in a freighted way. They were shocked, I bet, but who cares.

"How did you do that?" one man asked me.

"He took them down in the blink of an eye. First, they were standing, and now they are all dead." Another said.

I saw some blood on my hands, and I licked it up. It tasted disgusting. Bandits don't eat enough fruits.

"So, who is next?" I looked at them all- so scared, so afraid. Good, they fear me. I hope that I can just get Claire and leave then.

Suddenly, I felt something hit me, sending me flying into a crate. "Ouch. Well, that hurt." I thought to myself. Why is it that nothing can be easy just once for me? Why do I have to deal with people trying to beat the shit out of me?

That hit felt familiar. I looked over at the dead man walking. A guy holding a large club in his hand. He looked like a caveman.

"Why the Hell is he naked?" I thought.

"Well, I think you met Honger before. He helped us 'acquire' your little friend. He is well behaved when we can tame him, but without any restrictions, he is just a mindless killing machine." The guy who led this sorry group said.

"I hope you know that now none of you are leaving this place alive, right?" I said in a low tone.

"Well, we'll see. After Honger is done with you, we will proceed to sell your friend and buy supplies for our group. Maybe we will rough her up first, though, seeing all the trouble that you are going through to help her." He grinned and laughed out load. The other men began to laugh too.

I hate when people get too cocky and believe that they can do whatever the Hell they want.

"This is going to be fun." I thought as I cracked my knuckles.

I ran at the ugly man-beast before me, and before he managed to hit me with his club, I ducked out of the way, and instead aimed for one of the other men. I jumped up and closed in my leg before extending it as my foot made contact with his head, which broke off his spine the moment I kicked him.

After taking that weakling out, I saw the clubber coming at me. He aimed the club at me, but I dodged the blow, and instead hit his hand. He dropped his arm. As it dangled, I jumped up and head-butted him in the jaw. Once, I made it back on the group, I swiftly jumped out of the way as a man tried to shoot at me.

I charged at him, hitting him in the leg, breaking it, and sending him flying with an elbow to the head. Although, I stepped back when I saw Honger with his club coming at me. No matter what I did this guy was coming straight for me. Damn it! I hate fighting stupid people (especially, since he is naked).

I decided to use my speed. I ran before jumping onto a shelf, and once I landed, I looked around and noticed that there was only five men left: three bags of meat, the big brain, and the drooling beast.

"Great. I think, I know what to do."

I jumped down and ran towards the three guys, grabbing two of them, and tossing them into the third guy who went crashing through more crates.

"Why am I being careful here? Damn Roan! She always knows what to say for me to listen to her." I thought.

I stood up and looked ahead of me.

"Well, only two of you left. Who wants to go first?" I asked them.

The dork leader looked at me and grinned before turning the corner. Before I could chase after him, he returned with Claire in his right arm with a gun before him.

"You better give up or you will have to clean up some blood."

I stood still. Looking at Claire, I saw the fear in her eyes.

"Help me." She pleaded to me.

Before I could say anything, I felt another hit, but this time it was towards my legs. "Damn!" I fell and saw Honger behind me.

"No!" Claire screamed. I saw her try to run for me, but the man shot her leg and she fell.

DARKNESS. DARKNESS. DARKNESS!!!!

*"You know what to do." The voice said.*

*"No, I will not lose control of you." I said to IT*

*"You have grown weak from fatigue. I know you. Take revenge! Take them down."*

*A figure crowded over me. A dark figure.*

*"Leave me alone."*

32

*"How can you save her in your state? Take my hand. Take it!"*

*I looked up. I can't trust him, but IT'S right. I am tried. I am pissed. I am sick of this guy. I just want to get this fight over this.*

*I saw ITS hand lowered to me. I blinked. "I shouldn't. I know that, but Claire."*

*"Take it. Save the girl. Let me out."*

*I lowered my head. Years. That is how long it has been since I kept this thing inside me without an incident, but now. No! No! No! I can't. I won't. Not in front of her.*

RISING OUT OF THE DARKNESS.

I turned myself over and proceeded to break both of Honger's legs before having him fall on me. However, as he did so, I aimed my right fist at his mid-section before blowing a fist at it. He was sent flying through the roof and far away. The dork of a leader looked scared. I grinned before rushing over to him, and locking his head in my arms, I snapped his head, killing that son-of-a-bitch.

I breathed heavily. God, I need some rest. I looked over and saw Claire on the group. I walked over to her. I saw that she was bleeding, so I took a piece of cloth and tied it around her leg. She was asleep from the shock. That is good.

I picked her up, and I walked out of the building. I headed towards the tunnel to head back to Roan to get my damn supplies. I swear kids are too much trouble for their worth. I need to do some mediation. I have been skipping out on my usual routine because of the fricking heat.

I need to sleep. I need to eat. I need a damn break from taking care of other people.

"God, if you are punishing me, then why not just kill me. That would be a lot easier. Maybe, the old man has gone senile." I laughed at that.

Fin.

# 6.

## Just Moving Forward

I forgot how much walking that I did to get here. She said it was a quarter of a mile and yet it feels like two miles. I hate her sometimes. Why the Hell do I keep coming back to this shithole? Maybe, I needed to be in the presence of the damned before I feel all high and mighty. No, that's not it. Crap! Why am I here?

I kept walking and soon enough, I made it back towards the doorway. She closed it. Great, now I have to fricking knock.

I breathed, and as I took my step forward, I knocked on the door twice-loud enough for her to hear me. I waited and waited, but Roan did not open the door.

"Damn it, Roan! I am not in the fucking mood! Open the door or I swear that I will break it down!" I yelled at her.

At that moment, the door opened. She needs to learn when to cut some people some slack. I stepped out and saw that the place was a wreck (more so than it usually looks). I looked around and saw blood. Lots of blood. It led towards the counter area. I set the girl down on the ground and walked over to the counter. I slowly turned over the little separator, and as I did, I saw a pair of legs to my right.

"Roan!" I ran to her. She was breathing heavily. I could barely make out any features of her face with all the blood.

"Roan, can you hear me?" I asked her in a soft voice. "What happened? Who did this?"

I saw her eyes open-up, slightly. She looked around before looking at me. Her robotic arm was torn from her arm. Her two legs were gone as well. She was bleeding everywhere.

"Eilif... is... that you?" she asked as she left out a cough.

"Yes, it's me. What happened here?"

"Once, I let you pass those doors, a man came into the place and inquired about a missing girl. The one that you have with you. I told him that I did not see her here. He looked at me before taking his arm out and revealing an overgrowth hand. He looked at me, smiled, and said, 'I know that you are lying, but I don't care. I'm going to enjoy killing you. I will find her. You know the beast is always aware.' After he said that, he began to take me apart..."

Roan started to cry after that. "Shush. It's okay. I am here."

"He is after the girl. I have seen hatred before, and his eyes showed it. Those blank, dark eyes, full of evil, and full of nothing but hunger."

"What do you mean by hunger?" I asked her.

"After he did this...He then took my blood. Drinking it up like he needed a fix." She told me.

I stopped looking at her, and instead, looked out passed her. "It can't be." I thought. "He... No...but..."

I couldn't think. It made no sense. Not him! Not him!

I looked down at Roan. "Fuck, no! This can't be real."

"Roan, did his arm have any pictures on it?" I asked her frankly.

She looked up at me. "It had an eagle on it."

Her lips spoke those words, but I still refused to believe her. "It just can't be." I thought to myself over and over again.

"Stop thinking about it. Roan needs my attention. Stop it! Stop it!"

"Roan, I am going to get you some help." I went to get up, but she grabbed me by her one remaining hand.

"No, I am not going to make it. You and I both know that. Stop trying to act like a hero, it is not a good look on you. I know that you think that I don't know you, but I have known you long enough to say that you can't save everybody. You are a helper, and that is why I fell for you, but we were both different and stubborn people that were not going to settle down for anything. I just want you to remember that. Make me a promise."

"What promise?"

"That you will stick with this girl through everything. Be her hero. Be her somebody that she can rely on. Take care of her, and please, let her in. Let her into your heart. She will stick with you because you are you. Remember that you are who you are for a reason, and please, do not change that. Be yourself."

I started to cry. I couldn't help myself. She was the only one who could make me cry after all the shit that I went through. She was the one person that I told her things that I did not tell anybody else (but I refused to tell her everything that went on- I needed her to see me as me and not as anything else).

"It has been a while since I've seen you cry. I forgot how ugly you looked when you cried." She softly said to me.

I smiled at that. "Shut up, you have cried in front of me before, and I can say that you have a pretty crappy crying face."

We both laughed. We both needed this. The real us. The real world that we lived in. If just once, then we could be us together in this moment.

"I promise you, Roan. I will stay by her side." I finally said.

She smiled at me. "Good. You better keep that promise or I will have to come back and kick your ass." she said to me at last.

I felt her hand loosen. I saw her once hazel eyes fall, and then she was gone.

Silence. Utter silence. I felt alone. I felt indifferent. I felt angry. I felt sad. I felt remorse. I felt hatred. I felt silence. Time is a bitch! It takes what it wants and tells us to suck it up and enjoy life, because before you know it, that precious time that you spent your life in will be gone. Time stands to lose nothing, only people stand to lose everything, unless you have nothing, and then you have nothing to lose from time except the possibility to find something to hold onto.

"I hate you!" I screamed at the top of my lungs. I screamed it over and over again. Why did she have to go? Why the Hell did she have to go? Why the... Why the... I lost my train of thought as I continued to cry.

DARKNESS, PURE DARKNESS

*"Do you see what has happened because you kept me here? You could have saved her, but you were too weak."*

*I felt a heavy mass towering over me. Not him, not now. I am not in the mood.*

*"What do you want?"*

*"You are pathetic. Crying over this THING! If she meant so much to you, then take me out." IT said to me.*

*I growled at it. "Shut up. You don't get the pain that I feel. You don't understand the pain that I always feel."*

*I felt IT grin, an evil grin. "You forget, I have been with you all your life. I have seen everything through your eyes. I know everything that you know. I own you!"*

*"If you knew everything, then you would have heard of what she said. Remember? The man with the eagle tattoo on an overgrown hand?" I told IT.*

*"You don't mean him, do you? He is dead. You know that he is. WE BOTH KNOW THAT HE IS!"*

*"Well, who else could it have been? How many people do we know that match that description?"*

*I felt nothing at all, but then I felt something.*

*I raised my head a little and looked at the floor where IT was standing.*

*"You're afraid that it is HIM, aren't you?"*

*"I am not because HE is dead!" IT screamed at me.*

*"You are afraid." I said in a sympathetic tone. I understand why IT is afraid. I am afraid too.*

*"You can leave." IT said to me.*

*"What? First you wanted me to let you out, but now, you want me to leave. You brought me here. You don't want to talk to me about this. You said it yourself. You know everything about me, right?" I asked IT.*

*"I don't want to talk about this. I still can't believe it. I won't bother you so deal with your own problems. Goodbye, Eilif."*

RISING OUT OF SOMETHING

I regained my consciousness. That was the first time that IT said my name. In all these years, IT never said my name before. I did not know what to make of this, but with IT in the control seat, I can't ask anybody else what to do. I hate that I have to rely on this body of mine to work for me. The human body is, and always was, meant to function on how it is made to function. We live off of our bodies, not the other way around.

I looked back at Roan and wiped away my tears. I had to do what I promised her, but first, I need to find a doctor in this crappy town to help with Claire's wound. Great, that will take forever. No medical building within this town. I sighed and got up.

I walked over to where I laid Claire's body, and I proceeded to lift her up before holding her like a bride. She looked like she was having a pleasant dream by the way her face looked. So unafraid. So carefree. So comforted.

"I will keep my promise to you Roan." I thought as I walked outside of the building.

TIME PASSING AWAY

I walked down the long, dirt and blood engrossed street. Nothing has changed about this place. The people care about themselves and that is the main problem. That is why this place has gone downhill. It was a place founded by the idea that you can do whatever you want and nothing bad will happen to you for it. With this decree, the people started up the time in good fortune, but it soon fell to shit. You see, you need a town in order to live in a place that allows you to do what you want. So, the only time that the people within this cesspool of human waste ever joined together was when they built the damn place. After that, though, it was every person for themselves, and that is what the problem is. When people go off of what they want and ignore everybody else, they miss out on living in the present. They learn to live, but only off of their own time, and as I said before, time does not care about us, it only cares about what we feel is our precious time. It steals what we have until there is nothing left. These people are the people that have nothing and are trying to find something to cling to, and that is why they are only for themselves. They believe that by letting people in, then they will lose further what they don't have

It's an endless damn loop. A loop that keeps playing over as time keeps turning. They want pleasure. Well, here it is, but in return, time will have to take some penance for it. There is no good, evil, happy, sad, or sin in this world. It is about fighting to hold onto dreams and lost people that are gone. We cling to the past because it held such success and promise. We fear the future because it holds nothing but mystery and the unknown. Finally, we hate the present because it holds nothing of either the past or the future, it just sucks up the reality that we live in, the time that we are losing, and the prospects of nothing and everything that we need to see for ourselves to make them real for us in the long run. We need constancy. That is what we all want.

I eventually stumbled into a building that looked abandoned. It was the seventh stinking building that I looked through. Anyway, I walked in and saw that a person was a least living here. The place was cleaner than the others.

I looked around. A couch. A few chairs. A fridge. A lamp. A desk. A few bottles of alcohol littered the floor.

"Great, a drunkard." I thought.

"Anybody here?" I asked out loud.

I didn't hear anybody or anything. As I turned to walk out, though, I heard a crash, and it was at this point a person came stumbling down the stairs.

When they finally landed, I looked at them. It was one of those "Counter-BY-Sets" that you hear about here and there. A person who is not just a mixture of a man and a woman, but also is a mixture of robotic parts and animal DNA. It was something that the Kingdom of Humania created a century ago. People felt different in their minds, and as a result, the doctors of the Kingdom decided to help along the process of transforming people into what they wanted to be. If they felt like they were a dog, then they would transform them into a dog-person. If they wanted to be a man instead of a woman, they would be transformed into a man. If they wanted to be half robotic and half animal, then they would be transformed into something that incorporated both. Eventually, people wanted to have children be what they wanted from birth, so the doctors of the kingdom created the "Mult-Birth Calcu-Transformation Machine". Again, the same story. If you wanted to make your kid into anything, you could- but within reason, of course. Though, what was reason within the kingdom, you could never tell after the incident.

Anyway, I am not the one who is worth telling this information, but I find it helpful to remember that shitty place.

As I looked at the person who fell, I saw as they stood up, that they had a lion's tail, two robotic legs, the bulk of a monkey, and the eyes of an owl. "Geese, another reject, maybe?" I thought.

The person looked up at me before speaking:

"Yes, what do you want?" the person sounded tipsy. Just my luck, another person drunk off their ass in this town.

"I need a doctor. This girl is hurt. She was shot in the leg." I told the person.

"Oh. Then you came to the right place, then. I am a doctor. The only one here, I guess. I haven't meant any others yet."

"That's because this town doesn't have any doctors. Do you know where you are?" I asked. There is no way a person would come here to be a doctor. When somebody dies here, they either leave the body to rot, burn the body in the street -which causes the place to smell like burning flesh - they release the caged animals to eat it up, they throw it through a woodchipper, or other people who have not eaten anything in weeks will eat it.

"Yes, I am in Bonterkide. I came here to be a doctor for those who are suffering. Well, I just started here a month ago, though, so I haven't had any patients yet."

I sighed. "Well, a new doctor is better than no doctor. So, can you help her?" I asked the doctor.

"Yes! Bring her here." She said with excitement in her voice.

I placed Claire down on a table and watched as the doctor got to work. I have to admit, the doc was experienced. It took less that ten minutes for the doc to find the bullet, take it out, clean up the wound, stitch it up, and bandage the wound. After the doc finished, I looked at Claire. She looked healthy. More healthy than she looked when I saw her.

"She is going to be fine. Nothing looked bad. Just keep her off of that leg for two days and then she can walk on it." The doc told me.

"Thank you, doctor."

"Oh. Please, call me Maggie." The doctor said.

"Okay. Thank you, Maggie."

I sat in silence after that. I watched as Maggie was cleaning her medical tools. Life seemed to slow. I had experienced a tone of garbage within the last three hours alone. Rescuing Claire. Fighting a group of bandits. Fighting an overgrown caveman. Finding Roan seriously injured. Hearing about Him. Roan dying. Finding a doctor for Claire, and now. Life drags on like it never stops.

I looked at Maggie. She was from a time that I knew of, but she was from this new time that I am living in now. What type of world is this. Technological advances. Medical advances and drawbacks. Corruption. Mass death. Shit after shit after shit after shit! I need to lay off the world sometimes, but it is hard when it sucks so much.

"Are you two from around here?" I heard Maggie ask me.

"No. I am from somewhere else. Claire here is from Yondaster." I told Maggie.

"Really, isn't that far away. What is she doing out here?" Maggie asked me.

"Her old man sent her out here to find her mom. Her ride was attacked, and I found her living in it."

"So, you offered to help her get home?"

"Yeah, I felt bad for her." I said to Maggie.

"That is the sweetest thing that I have heard in a long time. It is good to hear that there is still some good in this world." She said to me with a smile on her face.

"Sure. Whatever you say."

I just sat there in silence. I did not want to say anything, nor did I want to feel anything. My world has gone to shit, and for what. This child? For Claire? Why did I decide to help her? Have I finally lost what sense that I had? Am I just stupid? I want to know why life put this child in my care. I help people when they need it, but that is because of my birth, my stature, my bloodline. All bullshit! Everybody that I once knew is dead. Yet, Claire- despite all the odds- has lived by my side for a few days now. She is a strong kid; I will give her that. It is only good. She will need to be stronger in the future, for I feel that the future will be laid with more turmoil, bloodshed, and retarded people that think that they have the answer to life, on how to live, on how to prosper, on how to become rich, on how to become powerful, on how to make love, on how to be without being, and more. I don't trust people, yet I do. I find faults in people based off of nothing but how they act, but isn't that how we are supposed to judge people. No! Of course not! People are all so fucking special that no one should be judged for what they do!

I hate life. I hate people. I hate pointless banter, but most of all, I hate myself for noticing the pointlessness of everything (though, I guess that is another one of my grand faults).

"I am going to take a nap on your couch. Wake me up when Claire wakes up." I said to Maggie.

"Go ahead. I have some work to do before the day is over." She said as I laid myself on her couch.

"I don't trust people, yet I trust them. I must be crazy." I thought as I closed my eyes.

Fin.

# 7.
## Not Quite the Start

"Where am I?" I thought as I sensed something was wrong.

I looked around and saw nothing but darkness. "Why am I here?"

Nothing was moving. Nothing was moving. I felt nothing, only a pure sense of familiarity. Then, out of nowhere, I saw a glimmer of light in the distance. I walked towards it. I kept walking, but the closer that I got, the farther that the light left me. I was alone again.

Suddenly, I was in a room. It was rather large. Wood stained the whole room. I saw crosses on the wall. I saw candles burning. I felt a peaceful sensation around me- like everything was going to be okay. I haven't felt this peaceful in years.

As I looked around, I noticed a person standing by the front of the room. They were wearing a white dress. A pure image of what beauty is.

"Zoe?" I thought. It can't be her.

I walked closer to her. She was waiting here for me, and here I am, but so what? "Is she here? Am I real?" I thought. Nothing made sense right now, but I felt in pure bliss as I stood next to Zoe. She always knew how to make me feel better.

The sun shone through the pictured windows of the place. "We are in a church." This place is familiar to me, but why? Why is it so hard to remember what this place is? Think! Think! Think!

Wait. Is this THAT church? No, it can't be! I left it behind. I left her behind. Why are these memories coming now? I don't need them! I don't want them!

*One moment it was solely peaceful, and the next the darkness returned, but this time it came with a grotesque image. Zoe was in my arms bleeding from her stomach. She was dying. She was whispering something into my ear. Why can't I hear what she is saying? I need to hear what she said to me. Damn it! Let me hear her one more time.*

I woke up. It was a dream, and yet it was a memory. I was shaking on the couch. Why am I shaking so much? What was that memory for, and why now? Shit! I need to get myself together. Stop shaking!

I moved my hand to my face, and I felt tears on my cheeks. "I am crying! Why am I crying?" I felt my hands clench by themselves on my head. I was still shaking. I need to stop shaking. I don't need this right now. I have to think about Claire. I have to think about Claire.

I breathed in. I felt myself calming down. Life sucks. I can't ever sleep without a memory coming to me. When I was young, my grandmother told me to look out for nightmares. I found out fast that it wasn't the nightmares that got to you, it was what the nightmares represented. They were our memories coming to us in flashes or scenes. They were tormentors. They were truths that we all try to forget. Damn! I have to think about Claire.

I stood up. I felt stiff all over. It has been a while sense I slept on something remotely soft life a couch. I looked around and noticed that it was dark out. I slept through the rest of the day in this shithole. I glanced over at the table and noticed that Claire was still sleeping. Good. She needs it.

I walked over to her. Softly, I breathed in the air around me. It was a cold air. I forgot how cold it gets at night around here. When I reached Claire, I looked closer at her face. That soft, unafraid face that seemed so full of promise, so full of life. I noticed that she was holding herself. "She must be cold." I thought.

I took off my coat and placed it on her. At that point, her face softened even more. She looked so beautiful. I sighed. It is a shame that life is like this. Children who have to grow up too damn fast. Forget the idea of youth. It is all about being better than your parents. Better than all the adults that have wronged you. Being better than all the sucky people in this world that made your life Hell, and for which you want to outgrow them, outgrow the world, and be your own person, be your own self-worth, and be your own hero.

I can't stand living sometimes, but I am too weak to do anything about it.

I sat back down on the couch to sleep some more before the morning.

## TIME PASS ON THE DREAM OCEAN

I felt something warm on my face. I opened my eyes, and I felt the rays of the sun beat upon my body. It was a warming feeling that I haven't felt in a while.

I sat up and looked over at the table that Claire was on. She wasn't there!

"Where did she go, now?" I looked around and didn't see her anywhere downstairs, so I decided to head upstairs. I walked up the stairs to the second floor. As I did so, I heard a voice. Two voices? Then, I heard laughter. I rushed up the stairs and entered into a large lab of some sorts. Beakers lined the floors. Books lied on top of each table (of which, I only saw three). Papers. Liquids. Robotic parts. Many other things cluttered up this space, but over in the corner of the room, I noticed two people sitting at a table.

"So, that is where she went." I thought to myself.

I walked over to the two people that I saw. Maggie turned to me as I approached and smiled.

"Good morning, sleepy head. I was just talking to Claire here about how she was feeling." Maggie told me.

At that point, Claire turned around and looked at me. She smiled at me with those bright amber eyes of hers'.

"Eilif!" she said as she ran over to me and hugged me. I felt uncomfortable, but I allowed her to hang onto me. She needed it after what she went through.

"Hey, I see that your leg is better." I said to Claire.

"Yes, Maggie said that I should try to walk on it if I can, but if it starts to hurt, then I should stop and take a break. Isn't she smart?" Claire asked me.

"Yeah, she is." I said back to her in a gentle voice.

I looked down at Claire. Her eyes were staring at me. I didn't know what to feel or what to do.

"Damn! What does a person do in this situation?" I asked myself.

I placed my hand on her head and rubbed her hair around. It was soft. I wondered if this is what.... I don't remember anymore.

"Well, how are you feeling, Claire?" I asked her.

She looked at me and smiled. I couldn't resist that smile of hers'.

"I am feeling better now. I was scared that they were taking me somewhere bad, but then you showed up. I knew that you would help me." She said in a bright voice that was full of gratitude and love.

"Love…" I just looked straight ahead and looked through one of the windows of the upper floor. Why did I have that dream last night? It made no sense. It has been years since them. Decades even, and I'm miles away from that place! Why did it come to my mind?

"I am glad that you are safe. Hey, thank you Maggie. How can I ever repay you?" I turned my attention to Maggie as I spoke.

She looked at me as she got up from her seat. She walked over to me and placed her hand on my arm for some reason. She looked straight into my eyes. I can't stand when people get this close.

"Just keep this girl safe. If you ever need anything, then you know where I am." She said to me as she walked over to one of her cluttered tables covered in junk and worthless materials.

"You're staying here?" I asked her. Though, I figured the answer.

"Yes. I need to stay here to help people who are suffering. You taught me that lesson. When a person is willing to go through so much to help somebody else that they don't know and who are suffering, then I need to do my part as well. I'm a doctor!" she looked at me with a determined look in her eyes. I knew that look all too well. It was the same one that Zoe had. The one that she gave everybody who she looked at. She believed that helping people was a must, and that if you didn't, then you were scum. I suppose that she rubbed off on me.

I sighed. "She deserved better." I thought to myself. I have been doing that often. I think! I think! I think! Yet, I don't want to think. My grandfather was a person who believed that to live life was to be the center of it. He was always the main attention at parties, weddings, and any social gathering. Even when we visited him, he was always the center of the evening. I grew to see him as a man that I wanted to be, but my mother told me that I could never be like him. I gave up on that dream. Here I am thinking again! Stop fucking thinking! I want to get through this day without thinking anymore!

"Good for you." I finally said to Maggie. If she needed to believe that she was inspired by my actions then she could, but I could not stand it. "However, I am not the right person to admire for helping people. I hate helping people. I want to just be by myself and live how I want to live. I want to walk. I want to look at life. I want to be away from people because they bring to many shitty memories for me. People, in my opinion, are scum and assed-tight pigs that deserve everything that is coming to them. Yet, I can't stop helping people. It is in my nature to help people. I have been created to help people. I can't live, function, or think without the very thought of doing something good for somebody else. I hate it! I hate it, but I can't help it. Do you see what I mean? You can look up to me as an example as much as you want, but I can't stand people who do that and don't understand what that person is thinking, so here it is." I finished my speech to Maggie.

I didn't care if she slapped me. If she hit me, screamed at me, or walked away from me. I didn't care one bit, but she just stood there looking at me. "Why is she staring at me? I don't want to deal with this crap."

Suddenly, I felt somebody touching me. I saw Maggie hugging me. "What the Hell is she doing?"

"I feel so sorry for you." She said to me in a whisper.

I looked at her. She was shaking just as Claire was shaking. Damn! What is with me and allowing these shaking women to break me down to a pile of weak trash that belongs in the incinerator?

"Don't." I said as I gently pushed her off me. I turned around and walked towards the stairs. I looked back only to see Claire looking at me with a worried look on her face. "Shit! Now, I made Claire worry about me. I don't need this."

I walked down the stairs and decided to wait until Maggie said it was fine for me to take Claire.

TIME PASSES BY ON THE SELF

I sat on the couch thinking again. Why am I an idiot when it comes to women? I can't stand them, yet I can't stand to hurt them or to yell at them. I have no problem in killing a man. I have no problem in threatening a person. I have no problem when it comes to anything brutal in life (though, that is against my will, just how it always is). Why am I so concerned with protecting innocent people? No one is innocent, I know that. If everybody is innocent before proven guilty them the opposite arises too. Everybody is guilty before proven innocent. Who are the innocent, anyway? I know of people who have been sent to prison over something so small and had parts of their lives taken from them. They were innocent, sentenced to be guilty, and them proven innocent. It is the same for other people. I heard of this person who was from a bad home- a home filled with druggies and stoners- and as he grew, he was labeled the same as his. A boy born innocent and sentenced as a guilty person before ever being condemned such. He started selling drugs to people but was never caught. It wasn't because he was that good, it was because that his whole family was a part of the towns revenue system (meaning, that they made the largest share of money towards the city). He was safe, not from his own actions but by those of the city itself. Some of the other people who condemned him and his family, were eventually jailed for skipping out on payments on cars, houses, and even on smuggling charges.

That is the society that thrives today. An innocent person is no different than a guilty person. We all kill. We all steal. Some a little, others a whole Hell of a lot, but in the end, it comes down to who condemns us. Our peers. Our people. Our world. We are the destitute. We are the forgotten. The living of the unlived. The survivors of the world that passes us by. That is what an innocent person can skip in life based off of what we consider innocent.

I hate life. I hate myself, but as I keep reminding myself, I am too much of a wet-assed-bitch of a person to take care of my own issues. I thrive on issues, yet I hate issues. I prefer things to be simple, but that is too much to ask in life.

I stopped my train of thought. I needed to stop thinking of pointless ideas that don't mean anything to me. To other people, maybe, but to me, they do not mean shit.

I heard a noise coming from the stairs. I looked up and saw that Maggie was leading Claire down the stairs. They both had smiles on their faces. "Why can't I smile so naturally?" I asked myself.

"Hey." Maggie voiced herself to me.

I nodded.

They walked up to me, and I saw that Claire was carrying a small bag over her shoulder.

"I gave you and Claire some supplies for your journey. It won't last that long, but it should last about four months." Maggie said to me.

"Thank you for everything that you did for us. How do I repay you?" I asked Maggie.

She leaned in and whispered into my ear:

"Just keep her safe. I mean it! She is a good person, and I see that you care about her, too." She backed away from me, and all I did was nod. I couldn't say anything else to that.

I looked down to Claire before kneeling down to her height. I looked into her amber eyes that shone like the light of a promising future.

"Well, are you ready to go? It is a long journey." I asked her.

She shook her head. "Yes, I am ready. I can't wait to get home!" she squealed out.

I sighed. This kid has no idea what she is in for, and yet, I am still trying to help her. Why?

I turned and began to walk out the door with Claire by my side. As we were walking out of town, I looked behind me and saw Maggie waving at us. I pointed to Claire, and she waved at Maggie. I just looked back.

I am glad that we are leaving this town. I never wanted to spend more than a few hours here and yet I spent a whole day and a half here. I hate how life changes in front of you. I made a plan and life said, "You know what? I see your plan, and I have a better idea. How about instead of doing what you want, I instead make it so that the girl you have is kidnapped, almost sold, is shot, and needs medical attention? How does that sound. Good? Good."

I hated... I hated... I hated... I don't know what to say any more about what I hate.

I remember a long time ago that I read a poem that rang like this:
*"And here I suppose that I am mute,*
*Because what I am is nothing new,*
*And I am just a fool to be so costly*
*When the way I hate lies in the lust of knowing."*

Poetry, right? Who would have thought that I knew poetry. Another secret out, I guess, but I could hardly care at this point. I am stuck here because I am bound by a bond that cannot be broken. A bond that won't allow me to end it all. A bound of boundless inequality. Fuck! Shit! Crap! Stop thinking! Stop thinking!

I looked over at Claire and saw her looking ahead. She was excited about the future. Why was that? I wanted to believe that something might happen. That something might change, but I knew the truth. People. Life. The Universe. Everything doesn't change, it only appears through our eyes that things change because somebody else is making it change. A person tears down an old building. Change! A star is blown out by itself. Change! The universe is too massive and there are too many universes. Change! We crave change, yet we fear it. We want truths, but we attempt lies. We want love, but we attempt contentedness. We want knowledge, but we settle for stupidity. Everything is the opposite of something else, but also, it is the same as itself. Nothing is different, yet everything is different. A paradox, I suppose, but I am no scientist. They died out. Humanity died out.

Yet here I am. A human helping a human. A person helping a person. Bringing darkness towards light and taking it back as well.

"I hope that I can finally be something that I can be. I don't want to be the me that I was made to be." I thought to myself before my thoughts faded into my walking.

Just walking. Just walking.

Fin.

# 8.
## Something for the Popper

The kingdom of Humania settled into a new age of contemplation. People became aware that this age would mean some changes, and that these changes would foster a new growth for the nation. The very presence of the military faded from the minds of the people. The original sense of the kingdom faded as this became the new standard, the new norm. Yet, life went on as usual within the confides of the kingdom's walls. People worked for the foundation of the kingdom, and the kingdom stood for the protection of the citizens and their individualities that fostered such brilliance. However, soon the new standard became a problem for the people. The military took from them money, supplies, and even its own people. Nobody knew the meaning of the kingdom's sudden shift, but it was of little value. People worked, people lived, and the kingdom grew and thrived.

Then, sometime within the past, a new threat arose. Something that threatened the peace and prosperity of the nation. Some new force like nothing ever seen before. The people grew restless, refused to work, and sought to keep to themselves. Fights broke out in the streets daily. Life as the citizens of the nation knew it was falling apart before their eyes. What occurred? A virus? A revolution? Nobody knows for sure, but this incident caused the kingdom to begin to lose its footing. The once great kingdom of unity, equality, community, and growth was failing before the eyes of the world. The military and the rulers of the kingdom sought to end this outbreak…

PRESENT:

We have been walking now for a few hours. I kept a steady pace, but I looked behind and saw that Claire was struggling to keep up. She was limping on one leg. Obviously, her right leg was bothering her, but she wouldn't say anything to me about stopping. Why?

"Let's stop here and rest." I said to Claire.

She nodded at me, but I could tell that she was thinking of something. "Why is she not talking to me?" I asked myself. It was weird. I thought that we were getting along better. Well, if she wants to ignore me all the way to Yondaster, then she can for all I care. Why do children have to be so stubborn when they want to be? I don't get it.

I sat my bag down on a rock that I found, and I sat on the ground. There was grass around for both of us to sit on away from the main roadway. She sat down a few feet away from me. Still not saying anything to me. "What is going on in her mind?" I questioned myself for the second time today. "God, why do I have to get stuck with a silent kid? I mean, if I am going to spend a year with her, then the least she could do was talk to me. She could annoy me. She could worry me. She could even ask me a thousand questions that I would eventually yell at her for, but she is just sitting there." I sighed.

If she wants to be quiet, then she can be. She has the capabilities to do so.

TIMES PASSES

We started back on the round about an hour ago. The sun was slowly descending. Good! Go back to your cave and leave me be. I hate the sun! I hate the heat! I hate the brightness! I sighed. All I do anymore is complain. Well, I am good at that, at least.

I looked back at Claire from time to time to make sure that she was still behind me and not lagging. Every so often when I looked backed, I would see her staring at me in a blank stare. At least she is acknowledging my presence. She seemed alright besides that staring, so we continued onward.

Night began to fall. I need to find a good place to sleep, because if I can't sleep tonight, then I swear I will kill somebody. I need my sleep. If a band of bandits try to steal any of my belongings, or try to steal Claire, then I will kill them. No one messes with my sleep and lives. If you don't believe me, then ask…wait, I killed that guy. Never mind.

"Hey." I began to say to Claire. "We are going to camp out for tonight. Follow me."

She nodded and followed behind me. I found a small clearing behind some large trees and a few bushes. This would make for a good cover for us. Shit! That means I can't make a fire tonight. Whatever, I'm doing what I want to do. If somebody shows up, then they better keep on walking or else.

I sat my things down. I looked at Claire before heading off into the neighboring woods to find wood to start the fire.

I pushed passed bushes with my hands. I didn't believe in using knives or other survival methods to live out in the world. Everything that I need is in my bones as a human. We were born hunters and survivors. We then decided to neuter ourselves of the gifts of life, and instead, we focused on trying to make our lives less stressful, less exciting, and less pain ridden by using technology to make ourselves lose the lives that we were supposed to always have. Looking back, I blame everybody. They were idiots beyond idiots. They suffered brain tumors and tried to inflict that same tumor on everybody else. Sadly, though, they succeeded. I am but one of the last few people who know what it means to live with the sense that the past was better off than us because they were ruining everything because they did not know that they were ruining everything. They were healthier because they did not know the idea of being healthy. They thrived on life because they did not know anything more than life. There were problems, but they were hidden under the surface. Then, sometime later, those issues were unearthed, and all Hell broke loose. People who claimed to know what to do wrote about it, and as a result, people followed what they wrote. Life was better back then because it was about living life. Keeping to yourselves and thinking about your community. We lost that. We lost everything when we began to realize the fragments of everything that was hidden from us for centuries.

Anyway, I grabbed some branches and headed back to the fire. Claire was still there. She was just sitting there, staring at nothing but the ground. She is starting to worry me, but I stayed focused on making the fire so that she would not freeze to death.

I started the fire with matches. I know! After everything that I said about our natural survival skills, I am using matches. Well, I have always used them. I don't need to explain myself to myself.

"God, I am losing it. I guess that my old man was right after all." I thought to myself as I laughed a little.

Claire noticed me laughing and looked up at me. I saw her amber eyes stare into mine. She was intently staring at me. I feel somewhat better that she is at least looking at me, but damn, those eyes of hers' are so big when she stares at people.

"What? Is it crazy to think that I find some things funny?" I asked her is a harsh tone. After ignoring me all day, I was a little pissed off at her.

She shook her head back and forth. "No." she said to me.

That was the first word that she said to me today. Damn! I am making her nervous again. God, why do you do this to me?

"I am sorry if I upset you back at Bonterkide. I didn't mean to make you feel upset in anyway." I finally said.

She looked at me in a confused way.

"I am not upset at you. You are the nicest person that I have meant, Eilif." she said to me with a smile on her face.

"Then, why have you been ignoring me all day?" I asked her.

She opened her mouth to speak, but then she closed it. She opened it again and did the same thing. Damn! Why can't people make up their own minds on whether they are going to answer somebody's question or not?

"I was just thinking about how I got here." She said flatly to me.

"How you got here?" I repeated her answer.

"Yes. I was just thinking how I went from my home to the stagecoach, to go on a long journey, be attacked by bandits, and then rescued by you." She finished before staring-off into the fire.

She started to shake again, so I took off my coat and handed it to her. I felt bad for her. Just a kid trying to find her mother all because her father doesn't want her. I mean, if you are going to send your daughter on a half a year journey to find her mother, then you would send her with an escort, or at least, a trusted friend to accompany her. No, this was about getting rid of her. For what reason, though, I do not know.

I reached into my bag and brought out a can of soup. I carefully boiled it over the fire to cook the inside before laying it on a cold rock to allow the can to cool down before placing the can above the fire again. An old trick that I learned a long time ago. I pulled out a spoon and handed both the soup and spoon to Claire. She took them and began to eat.

Meanwhile, I just stared into the fire. The flames danced around in the same yellow, red orange tinted way. Swaying in the cold night as a dancer would do. The flame was mesmerizing.

"Aren't you going to eat anything?" I heard Claire ask me.

"I will. Later though. I am going to stay up and keep watch tonight." I said to Claire.

She handed me the soup and spoon. I waved my hand.

"No. You go ahead and finish it." I said to her.

"I am full, and I don't want it to go to waste." She said back to me.

I took the soup and spoon, and I began to eat some of it. I looked back at Claire who was staring at me with a smile on her face.

"I am glad that I met you, Eilif." She said to me.

I looked at her. Why would she say that out of the blue? I mean, I am eating canned soup by a fire with her watching me, and the first thing that comes to mind is that she is glad that she met me? What the Hell is going on in her mind tonight?

I took another spoonful of soup. It was cold, but I didn't care in the least.

"Why are you saying that? Don't you have anybody that you think may miss you?" I asked her.

She looked down into the fire. Thinking. Thinking. Thinking. She raised her head and her eyes looked directly into mine. I saw tears that were forming in her eyes. I felt bad for her.

I moved over to her, and bent down on the ground to her eye level before saying:

"Do you want to talk about it?" I asked her.

She looked at me. Still crying. Eventually, though, I saw her blink and then she placed a hand in mine.

"I am scared." She whispered to me.

"Why are you scared?"

"I want to think that I have people that care for me, but I never knew my mother, my father was always too busy for me, and I have no friends. I don't know why I want to go home, but I do. I want to go home." She broke down crying.

I saw her shaking. I saw her tears rolling down her face. I could feel the pain that she felt. I felt bad for her.

I grabbed her and forced her into a hug. I heard a gasp from her, but I didn't let go. She was hurting, and I know what that feels like. The pain is deep inside just trying to find a way to escape. I heard people say that too much stress will kill you, but I know that pain- deep pain- will kill you worse. It builds up over time, and then comes out when you don't know when it will. Sometimes, it comes out as anger. Other times, it comes out as tears. As chokes that restrict your breathing. As a force that feels like it is pushing down on you and making you feel confined, which causes a person to shake, to hyperventilate, to ask for help on what to do. It comes as tears that darken your eyes as red. Yet, the worst of it is that the pain sometimes will come so strong that you need to hit something, or someone, to get rid of the pain. I used to hit myself for messing up. I would wake up the next day where big fist-sized light green bruise marks would be. They would stay with me for weeks on end before fading away (that is until I did it again). At that point, when you hurt somebody or yourself, that is the point where you realize that the pain will only go away if you were to go away.

So, people shoot themselves. Some used poisons. Some overdose. Some jump off of a building or bridge. Some cut themselves. While others think of other ways to kill themselves.

Pain is pain is pain is pain. That is what I know the best.

I held onto Claire tightly. She kept crying, but her shaking stopped. That is a good sign. I kept holding onto her until she spoke up:

"I think that I am done crying."

"Are you sure?" I asked her.

"Yes." She said back to me.

I slowly let go of her. I saw that her eyes were red and that her cheeks had a glare to them from the fire because of the wetness of her tears. She used my coat to wipe the wetness away. I didn't care. She needed to calm down and relax, I understood that.

"Thank you." She said to me.

I nodded. I went to stand up, but I felt her hand holding onto my mine. I looked back at her, and I saw that she was staring into the fire away from me.

"Can you sit with me for a little while?" she asked me.

I looked at her. "Sure." I spoke.

I sat down next to her. We were both silent for a long time. The silence was deafening. I felt uncomfortable. Is that why I think to myself all the time? Am I afraid of being silent? I guess that I am just a wimp as anybody else, then. "God! I am so weak." I thought to myself.

"Do you want to talk about it?" I asked her the same question.

She continued to look into the fire. The question just seemed to melt into the flames. I felt that she would just keep quiet for the rest of the night, so I decided that I wouldn't say anything else.

"I don't feel like I have a home anymore." She said.

I looked at her.

"Why do you feel like that?" I asked her.

"I am far away from home. I was attacked. I was kidnapped. I never found my mother. I don't feel that people need me. I feel that I am just drifting every-where and nowhere at once. Life seems to pass me by while everybody else is liv-ing as if nothing is wrong." When she finished, I heard her sigh out loud.

I looked from her to the fire, and then back again to Claire.

"Life passes by whether people notice it or not. People know that, but they choose to live in the moment. Survive one day at a time. They worry about their own lives, and they forget what matters, sometimes. People do live life, but they understand what is wrong with this world. You are a bright kid for thinking about this. Life hurts, but we live on as if it were just another day. That is how people live. Problems do not exist in their minds, but only the idea of living for tomorrow." I said to her.

She looked at me. I saw that her eyes widened with what I said. I didn't know what else to say. I don't want to lie to her. I don't want to hurt her. I want her to find what she needs to survive in life. To live one day at a time.

"You're right." I heard her say. "I guess that I need to look at life as a day that means new beginnings than endings."

"I guess you could look at it like that." I said to her.

"I just feel lost because I lived somewhere else for my whole life, and then I was told to leave to find my mother. I feel alone and separated from what I know. From what I am used to doing every day. I miss my old life." Claire said to me.

I can hear the pain in her voice as she says this. I know what… I know what… I just want to say that how she feels right now is how I felt before. I lived life. I still am, but as a different person that what I was.

"Sometimes, when a person feels separated from something that they knew for the longest time, it can be frightening, but think of it as a story. When one chapter ends, another chapter begins. Another section of life is born from change. It sounds crazy, but I was always afraid of change for the longest time." I said to Claire.

She looked up at me in surprise. "Really?" she asked me.

"Yeah. I felt lost from what my life started as. I was used to living, sleeping, eating, and just spending most of my time in one place, but then one day that changed. I had to move on. I never wanted to grow up, but life has different plans for people. I finally accepted my life as what it was turning into when I read a book about the First Red Scare in Russia during the early years after the First World War. The book talked about this person who had to leave their home in Russia because Jews were being threatened by the Russian government. Their family left for America. The person stayed behind for medical reasons. It took the person a whole year before they could enter the United States and see their family. They were smart. They were brave. Yet, they were afraid and worried about being accepted within the U.S. I decided after reading that book that life goes by in a similar way."

I looked at Claire and she smiled at me. She reached out and hugged me.

"Thank you." Claire said to me. Then, she just stayed close to my chest for a while.

Eventually, enough time passed when she let go and I placed some more wood into the fire. She looked happy and held a smile on her face. "Good. She is happy now. Maybe, I can get some sleep now." I thought to myself.

I settled myself down on my bag in order to fall asleep. Just as I closed my eyes, I felt something move close by me. I opened my eyes and saw Claire standing over me. She looked down at me with bright eyes. I could tell what was on her mind.

"Fine. You can sleep by me tonight, but I don't want this becoming a damn nightly thing." I told her.

She nodded and sat herself next to me.

"Goodnight." She said to me.

"Yeah. Okay." I told her.

I closed my eyes again. I feel that I am becoming weak. A few days ago, if a person spilled their life before me, I would have yelled at them, and would tell them to shut the fuck up. Yet, now, I feel that I am changing. It has been years since I felt like this. A person who is willing to give people advice. To be by their side. To comfort them. Sure, I help people, but not in this way. I guess that the old geezer has plans for me yet.

"I hate it when you're right, but here I am. I am changing just as you said that I would. God, if only I didn't make that bet with you. I'm going for broke now." I thought to myself.

Fin.

# 9.
## A Passage of Point

*"Where am I?" I thought.*

*I looked around and I was in a black void. "Not, again. Why am I having so many memories?"*

*"This isn't a memory. It is your death!" I heard a voice say.*

*"Wait. I know that voice! It can't be!" I started to shake. I haven't heard that voice in a long time. It was low and full of evil that I could hardly stand it. That voice! That damn voice! It can't be him!*

*"Why struggle to fight it? You know my voice and what I am capable of." The voice laughed.*

*I knew that laugh. No! It is not him! I am just imaging everything. He is dead! I know that he is dead.*

*I was breathing heavily. I hate when I start to breath heavily. I can't stop myself once it starts. Usually, I can just break a tree or a rock, or try to meditate, but not now. This voice was coming from everywhere, I felt the voice on my neck. I felt the haunting stink that the voice made me feel. No! No! No! This is not happening. I am just imaging everything.*

*"I assure you, my old friend, that I am real. How have you been? I see that you are doing well." The voice said to me.*

*"No! I know that you are dead. I saw it with my own eyes. You can't be here!" I shouted.*

*I started to crumble on the inside. This person. No, this creature was just a nightmare that I am having. He is NOT here! I know that this is not real.*

*"Why doubt what you feel? I know you well enough that your gut feelings are always correct."*

*"Stop talking to me like you are here! You can't be here. You can't be alive. I won't allow it!" I screamed at the voice.*

*"That hurts me. I came by to say 'hello' to an old friend of mine and this is how I am treated after all of these years."*

*"Well, you said hello. Now, go!" I said to the voice.*

*"Feisty! Just how I remember you. Good to know that things haven't changed since I have been gone."*

*He said to me.*

*"Go!" I screamed before breaking down on the dark floor underneath me. I was crying a little bit. I needed this to end. "Please, go. I can't stand seeing you."*

*"Very well, but this is not the last time that we will meet. I will call upon you to finish what we started. Until then, I hope that you and Claire have a good journey." The voice said before fading out.*

*"What? How do you know about Claire? How?" I screamed into the blackness.*

*I just sat there. I didn't want to move. "He can't be real. I know that he is not real. He can't be real."*

*I was shaking. I was breathing heavily. I was crying. I was falling apart. Look at me, a man falling apart.*

*Deeper I went into myself. I was falling to pieces. I felt myself in a new void. A darker void than before.*

*"Go away. I can't stand seeing you." I said in a whisper.*

*"He is alive. You cannot doubt that anymore, and neither can I." IT said to me.*

*"I can't take this. Why now? Why after so many years?" I questioned to myself.*

*"The Reaper is cunning. I should have known better. I should have taken care of him myself then allowing you to stay in control. You are too weak. Too emotional. Let me out! I can take care of him and everybody else that is in our way. I need to take care of them!" I heard IT scream.*

*I stood up and clenched my fists. I turned around and stared off into the distance before I noticed the sunken-in eyes that stared at me. I breathed in and spoke calmly:*

*"I will never let you out. Not after last time. Not after what you did to*

*them all. I have strength because of the others and because of myself. I can handle myself. I don't need you, so stay in here and don't bother me." I told IT.*

*"Why you little bastard! I should kill you right now if I wasn't stuck in here. I would rip you apart and then kill the girl. She deserves it after making us go through all that trouble." IT said to me with a low growl.*

*"Her name is Claire," I said to IT ", and before you go and say anything else, I want to let you know that you are never getting out of here. I will not let you." I shut my mouth after that.*

*I turned around and began to walk out of the void. I walked and walked and walked. I slowly saw light, and as I reached it, I turned around to look back into the void. I could still see those sunken eyes. I turned and walked out.*

I awoke. It was just morning. I saw the sun slowly rise over a few mountain tops to our right. The bright yellow of the sun telling me that I was waking up to a new day of excitement.

I sighed and lowly stood up. I looked around and saw that Claire was still sleeping. "Good. I didn't wake her up." I thought.

I went towards the woods and decided to pee on some bushes. I needed a distraction before starting today. More walking and walking. I needed some time to realize that.

I went over to my bag, and I grabbed a package of meat. I took a knife and cut some thin slices of that meat before starting up the fire again. I slowly set the thin slices of meat over the fire to cook. As I was setting up the pieces of meat, I saw Claire move out of the corner of my eye and wake up.

She looked over at me and smiled. She waved at me. I needed that wave today. I had a crappy night.

She walked over to me and sat down on a rock across from me. She just stared into the fire again. I guess that she is still recovering from the talk that we had last night. I understood that. People need quiet sometimes. I enjoy it. Maybe, a little too much. That is why I started to talk to myself. You are your own worst and best friend. A person of a person of solitude.

"Good morning, Eilif." She finally said to me.

"Morning." I said back to her.

"What are you making?" She asked me.

"Some bacon. I thought that we could eat before leaving for another day of walking."

Her smile faded. I saw this. I understood how she felt. Walking is troublesome, but I have been doing it for years and years now, so it didn't bother me as much anymore. Yet, she was young. She wasn't used to walking every day. Walking a hundred or so miles a day. I felt bad for her, for all the young kids of today. They grew up with cars to drive them where they wanted. No parent. No guardian. They just got into a car and said where they wanted to go, and before they knew it, they were there. The simplicity of the invention caused many children to skip walking. They drove. They had money. They fostered attitudes of unhappiness because of their easy lives. I knew better, but they didn't. I felt bad for them.

"Why so down?" I asked Claire.

She looked up at me. "Nothing." She began to tell me. "I just hoped that we could drive more. I am tired of walking."

I sighed.

"Yeah, I know. I have been walking for so long that it doesn't bother me. I guess that your legs must be hurting. Right?"

She nodded. I only looked at her face before going back to watching the bacon sizzle. It was starting to brown up. Only a few more minutes before we can eat some.

TIME PASSES TOWARDS THE STORY

We have been walking for the last two hours. We had eaten everything, and I cleaned up. We packed up, and then we were on our way.

I looked up into the sky. I saw white clouds lining the sky. They were making shapes all over. (I could have sworn that I saw one that looked like a pie that was baking cookies. My dumb imagination at work again).

Everything was rather peaceful. The wind blew a gentle breeze around us. The sun was staying behind the mountain tops, and I was rather happy for a change. I felt better today than I have felt over the last few years of my life. Life felt good for some reason.

Suddenly, I heard a shot. I stopped in my tracks and listened. Claire stopped a few feet in front of me. She looked back at me with a confused look on her face.

"Damn! Whenever I start to feel good, something comes along and ruins it. Fuck you, old geezer!" I thought in my head.

I kept listening. I definitely heard a shot. It wasn't that far, either. I kept listening for another one, but I didn't hear a thing, so I started to walk forward again. Claire just fell in line behind me as I kept walking.

We kept walking for the next hour, and nothing seemed to take place. No sound. No weird noises. No other people. I started to feel something watching us. People are known in these parts of the Hangstar Pass. Why is it that no one is here now? Something is here. I know that, but what is it?

Shit! I hate that people can be scared away by something so easily. People are weak.

I kept walking with Claire behind me. I heard nothing. No birds chirping. No wind blowing. No leaves moving. No people talking. It was all so eerie. The sun was up, but this place was deserted. Nobody around here. Something is wrong.

TIME PASSES TOWARDS A BRIDGE

We eventually made it past the densely wooded forest on either side of us, and we were just reaching the Hangstar Pass Bridge. A fairly new structure that was made within the last thirty years for travelers to drive on or walk on. In the past, it was used as a trading center to sell food, technologies, medicines, books, and anything else that you could think of. Mostly legal things to say the least. It was a peaceful place, but now there was nothing. It was just the bridge and the abyss that stared at you from the far side underneath the bridge.

It was odd not to see people. I had traveled this way around three years ago and everything was still the same. Why is there nobody around here? What happened?

"Well, whatever it was, it doesn't concern me right now." I told myself as Claire and I were nearing the opening of the bridge. As we did so, though, I saw that there was something at the opening of the bridge. It was large as Hell. Hairy too. It had one large horn that stuck out from the stop of its head. It looked like a lion with wings. Wait... no, it can't be.

I grabbed Claire by her arm, and we hid behind a large bush. I placed my hand over her mouth to keep her quiet.

"Don't make a single noise. That is something that we don't want to deal with right now." I whispered into her ear.

"Shit! Why did it have to be a Pixiu?" I thought to myself. "I thought that those things were extinct. Well, looks like I'm wrong, aren't I?" I sighed. This is not my day.

I looked out over the top of the bush to see the creature better. It was just moving on the bridge. I don't like when I run into people or creatures that just wonder around a place, not knowing what to do. It irritated me.

I ducked down again. "What the Hell am I going to do?" I asked myself. I looked around and saw nothing that could help me. It was just Claire, the Pixiu, and me. There was nobody else, and nothing that could help me.

I usually would not have any difficulty dealing with many things, but when it comes to one of the legendary creatures of lore, I have trouble with dealing with them. I hate how things are playing out.

"What is that thing?" I heard Claire ask me.

"It is a Pixiu. One of the legendary creatures from the ancient world. I haven't seen one in years." I answered her question.

"What is it doing here?" she asked me.

I shook my head. "I don't know, but you do not want to mess with one of these things." I said to her.

I was thinking about her question. Why the Hell would one of these things be here? Wait, duh, idiot. It is here because of how people traded things here. Of course! I'm an idiot for not thinking of it sooner.

Well, I hope that it has had its share of left-over goods because I am not going to stay here forever.

TIME PASSES: THE SUN SETS

Night had just fallen not long ago, but the Pixiu was still there. Why me? Why me? I hate life. I don't want to deal with this thing. They are a pain in the ass to deal with. Shit! Fuck! Shit! I hate this day so much.

Claire and I continued to hide behind the bush. The Pixiu had not noticed us. That is good at least. I don't need to deal with this shit today.

I looked over at the light mountain top and saw that the sun was finally falling over the last peak. Now just the night was here. The darkness. The breathlessness of the night. Just us and the Pixiu.

I decided to look over the bush again to see if the Pixiu was still there. I hope that it just flew away.

I looked up over the bushes and saw that it was on the bridge now. It was sniffing the ground, looking for more gold and wealth that was left behind. Such a greedy push-over. It can't deny what it was sentenced to do for the rest of its natural life. What is natural anyway? People are natural. Trees are natural. Lies are natural. The sun is natural. So, what makes something unnatural? People decide what is and isn't natural. Life keeps to itself- only getting involved when something was created that it did not create. Life has its own take on what is natural and un-natural. If life made it, then it is natural. People, however, say that what is not them, or is not what they have known for all their lives, is unnatural. For them, anything that they have not made or seen is unnatural. Contradiction! People are all hypocrites, and they all contradict each other. It pisses me off!

Yet, I stare at this creature and only think about one thing. It was made to do what it does, and that is all it knows, so if somebody comes around and tries to stop what it knows, the Pixiu will tear that opposing force apart. I've seen it.

The Pixiu is a creature that was made when it defiled some sacred act of the universe, and as a response to that, it is forever told to eat gold and jewels as food source. Yet, it can never release its feces because the universe closed its anus, thus making it so that the Pixiu will always be unsatisfied. So, it keeps eating and eating and eating, but will never get full. Poor bastard.

I looked back at that creature. It made a mistake and now it suffers for it. We all make mistakes, and we suffer. Yet, the ways that we suffer are crueler than some. We go to jail. We have our lives and time taken away from us. We are for-gotten by the world. We have our names forgotten, and thus we fade away. We are scorned by the society that we were once a part of. We are refused the same chances that other people have in life. Our choices create actions, and those actions define the rest of our lives. That is what sucks in life. We don't know how to forgive and to forget any more. My mother believed in the idea. To forgive someone is to allow that person's actions to be forgotten, and thus a new start can be made. They call it redemption. Forgiveness. Love the person that has wronged you. Bullshit! You are only wronged by one person in life, and that is your own pathetic self. We are all shitty people who can hide our own fears, mistakes, and lies in different ways. I hate people for lying to themselves. I learned a long time ago to stop that. It is unhealthy for a person to do that.

I sighed. We are all terrible, but we are all humans. So, what does that turn into, then?

I looked at Claire. She looked sleepy. I saw that her head was rested upon my chest.

"Go ahead and get some sleep. I will keep watch to make sure that we stay safe." I whispered to her.

She nodded and closed her eyes. I sighed. She needs to sleep. Tomorrow this thing better be gone, because I am not dealing with this thing tomorrow. I can't

"Well, let's see what happens, then. Shall we?" I thought to myself as I adjusted my body to a more comfortable position in order to stay awake for the rest of the night. "If you wake up Claire, though, I will end your life. Do you hear me?" I whispered out into the air.

Fin.

# 10.
## A Fight for Sacrifice

I stayed awake throughout the whole night. I felt stiff all over my body. I looked at the sun slowly rising over the small mountains. The leaves behind me were a bright red and orange assortment of colors.

I looked down and noticed that Claire was still sleeping on my chest. I gently placed my hands under her, and I slowly lifted her off me before setting her down on the ground. After placing her on the ground, I glanced over the top of the bushes to see about the Pixiu.

I saw the bridge and it looked empty. However, I don't remember the creature flying off during the middle of the night. I stayed up all night long, and I don't remember hearing any sounds being made.

Just as I was looking, I saw out of the corner of my eye the Pixiu leaning against an old shack that was built by the side of the mountain. It was sleeping. I sighed. At least it was out cold for now.

I turned my head to Claire. I bent down to her and shock her to make her wake up.

"What? What's going on?" she asked as I saw her eyes slowly flutter open.

"The Pixiu is sleeping. We are going to try and walk across the bridge before it wakes up." I told Claire.

Claire got up after hearing what I said. She grabbed my coat and I grabbed both of our bags. I slowly made my way out into the open. I walked a few feet away from the bush before turning around and motioning for Claire to follow me.

We walked slowly towards the bridge. The air was nowhere. The sun's heat was just barely noticeable. The water far beneath the abyss. The bridge was quiet. Even in the morning, life is silent.

As we were walking, I kept my eyes on the Pixiu. I made sure that the thing was not awake. I didn't need it to wake up. Just stay asleep and everything will be okay.

We made in onto the bridge. I allowed for Claire to go before me.

I looked at the brigde. It was a strong-structured bridge. It was made from steel and heavily designed from the old Golden Gate Bridge that used to thrive as the main connection of San Francesco before its collapse around thirty years ago. Although it was on a smaller scale, this bridge had the same red tint to it, and it had the same support beams and overall structure of the famed bridge. I never understood the mechanics behind bridge designs, and I do not care about it. That is useless information for me.

We were making good progress. We were about halfway across the bridge. I was switching my attention between walking forward and looking back at the Pixiu. Then, all of a sudden, I heard a shot.

"What? That shot sounds familiar." I thought to myself.

Shit! I hope that is not what I think it is. I turned around and saw a few bandits standing off into the distance.

"Hey! You and the kid better freeze right there. We'll be taking your valuables." The leader of the group said.

"Hey, watch out for…" I cut Claire off by placing my hand on her mouth. I shook my head at her.

I turned towards the guys, and I could clearly see the Pixiu starting to wake up. "They don't see the thing from where they are standing." I laughed as I thought to myself.

"What is funny?" one of the other bandit members asked me.

"Oh, nothing. Except, that you are all going to die." I simply said to them.

"That's it! Charge at them, boys." I heard the leader say.

As they started to run towards us, the Pixiu came into view and roared a loud roar. It looked at them men, and it started to devour them whole. I turned around to Claire and started pushing her to move forward.

"Go!" I yelled at her.

We started to run over the bridge. At that point, the Pixiu noticed us, and after stretching out its wing, it flew into the air at us. I saw that it was coming straight for us, so I grabbed Claire and through her to the other side of the bridge along with my two bags.

The Pixiu came down upon me and opened-up its mouth wide to show off its long sharp teeth.

"Shit! I forgot that this thing was part dragon head." I thought to myself as I was holding its jaw away from me.

This really isn't my fucking day. I struggled to find any way to grab onto this thing. It was big, but there was no good place to grab onto it. I got tired of holding its mouth open, so I just hit the creature in its neck. It stumbled back, and in that I managed to get up from its grip. I don't like fighting legendary creatures. They have hundreds, if not thousands, of years of natural fighting instinct in their bodies. I only have my life to talk about my fighting experience. These things piss me off too. They are so damn stubborn! They don't know when to quit.

"I guess that is the only thing that we have in common." I thought to myself.

The Pixiu charged at me. I jumped out of the way and instead grabbed it by its two tails and swung it around in a circle. "Damn! This thing is heavy." I thought, but I managed to spin the thing at least a few times before tossing it a few feet away, and into the steel post of the bridge.

It let out a large roar in pain. I was breathing heavily. This thing was both heavy and dangerous. I didn't need this after not sleeping for a whole night. God, I hate my luck. Wait, I have no fucking luck. Shit!

It got up and outstretched its claws and slashed at me. I moved out of the way for its first hit, but when I turned my head, I saw it coming down on me with its mouth. I felt a sharp pain in my shoulder. It was biting into me.

"AHHHHHHHHHH!!!!!!!!!" I screamed.

"Eilif!" Claire screamed in fear.

I felt it sucking me dry of something. I started to feel weak, but I was losing control of my mind. I feel into myself.

DARKNESS. DARKNESS. DARKNESS.

*"Let me out!" IT said to me.*

*"What is happening? Why do I feel weak?" I asked IT.*

*"This thing sucks the bad energy out of anybody that it bites, and I am nothing but bad energy! Let me out so that I can deal with this thing! You are obviously too weak."*

*I fell on the dark ground. I started to couch. I was losing my will. I felt the space grow shorter.*

*"No...(cough)...I can handle this. I don't need you." I said.*

*"You are a fucking fool. Let me out you weakling! It will kill both of us before it is done!" IT screamed at me.*

*I coughed. I couldn't stop laughing.*

*I feel to the ground on my face.*

*"I am not weak. I am not weak. I can do this." I said over to myself.*

*"You are risking both of our lives here! Not to mention the others. They all have options to live. Let me out!" IT said again.*

*I winced in pain. I started to feel myself fade away.*

*"No! I won't let it end like this." I slowly rose up.*

BACK TO THE BRIGHTNESS

I grabbed the Pixiu's single horn and broke it off. It let go of me and roared in pain. I grabbed its horn and stuck it into the front of its chest- just missing its heart. It screamed as it stumbled back. I was holding my right shoulder that was bleeding profusely.

"Shit! It took more blood than it should have." I breathed in and I stormed at the creature.

I pulled out its horn, and I proceeded to stab it over and over again. I watched as it was bleeding everywhere. I didn't care. I wanted this fight to end. I didn't care if it was illegal to do this. I wanted this to just end.

I kept stabbing it. I stabbed it. I just couldn't stop stabbing it. I was having too much fun. The Pixiu's blood was going everywhere, and I enjoyed every second of it.

Eventually, the creature fell to the ground. At this point, I took the horn and shoved it straight into its skull, and I watched as its eyes just dropped and it was dead.

I breathed heavily. I looked at the creature before me. I was all bloody. There were at least fifty stab wounds in it. I didn't care if it suffered as it was dying. That last hit was a mercy hit for it. The thing deserved that at least.

I bent down and licked up the blood from the body. I kept licking up the blood. It tasted so rich. So flavorful. I enjoyed every taste of it.

After licking up a good bit of blood, I stood up, and I smiled at what I did. I looked over to where Claire was standing. She was shaking. She looked terrified. My smile immediately dropped off my face. I wiped up the blood with my left arm, and I slowly walked over to her. I passed her and picked up both of the bags that were behind her.

I started walking away before I turned back, and said to Claire:

"Are you coming or what?"

She turned around and started to follow me. There was utter silence.

TIME PASSES

The rest of the walk neither one of us said anything to the other. It was just silence. Nothing but the sound of the birds in the air. The movement of the leaves on the trees from the wind. I felt bad for her to see that, but at the same time I didn't feel anything about it. She needed to see something like that at least once in her life. Kids need to learn about the hardships of life. Life isn't all great. Sometimes you have people who are always with you, and other times there is no one with you. You are alone. People- especially kids- need to learn to suck it up sometimes. Actually, kids are better equipped to deal with traumas than adults are.

Shit! Shit! Shit!

I looked at Claire and she had the same expression on her face from when we restarted our walk. It was a look of fear, confusion, and sorrow. I knew those feelings all too well. I have seen them on people's faces before. They are not all pretty. They are all full of blankness and heartless memories that need to be either forgotten or supplemented with better memories. Life sucks. It just sucks, sometimes.

Anyway, the walk continued-on for a while longer until I saw that the sun was going down. I noticed that there was a trail up ahead. It looked pushed back into a forest area, but it was slightly overgrown. It made for a perfect place to stay hidden from bandits.

"Hey." I said to Claire.

She stopped walking and looked up at me with wide eyes.

"We are going over there in that area to spend our night." I said to her.

She only looked at the area that I pointed at and then back at me. She didn't say anything. She only followed me.

Once we got behind the brush that covered up the old trail, I grabbed some nearby branches and placed them on the ground. I started up and fire and pulled out a can of beans from my bag. I was cooking the beans over the fire when

I decided to look over at Claire. She was just staring into the fire. She didn't look alive. She looked lost in thoughts. She looked lost within herself.

I sighed. I must have scared the shit out of her for losing my shit back there.

I looked at her and spoke in a caring voice:

"Hey, are you alright?"

She didn't move her head.

"Are you scared of me now?" I asked her.

She only nodded to my question. I was afraid of that.

"You don't have to be afraid. I just lost my cool back there."

She looked up at me and stared at me for the first time after the incident.

"Why...did... you do that to that creature?" she asked me.

"I had to. It was going to kill us." I said to Claire.

"No, I mean why did you have to stab it so many times and lick its blood from its body?" she flatly asked me.

I could tell that she wanted answers, but I didn't feel like she needed to know about that right now, or ever for all I cared.

Instead, I told her:

"They say that only by ripping off the Pixiu's horn and stabbing it with its own horn is the only thing that will kill it." I answered her first question.

"Then, why did you lick up its blood?" she asked me

That was tougher to lie about to her. I thought for a few seconds before answering.

"The legends also say that if you drink up the Pixiu's blood then you will be blessed with wealth and luck within your life."

She just looked at me. I hope that she bought that because I didn't want to answer her stupid questions anymore.

She finally said to me:

"Okay. Thank you for saving me and being honest with me."

She smiled at me. I missed that smile.

"You're welcome. Here have some beans for dinner." I handed her a bowl of beans. She ate them with a lavish look in her eyes.

"She must have been hungry." I thought to myself.

I ate my beans. I looked into the fire. I didn't like to lie to people. It has been a long time that I have had somebody who has relied upon me. Even back

then, when I lied to someone it was for a surprise or to just trick them, but now...
I don't know. I don't want her to know what I am. She deserves a better image of
me. I need to be something that she can look up to and say that I want to be like
that person. That she wants to try to be better than me. I talk about mistakes, but I
have a whole life worth of them. I regret many things in my life. I only live for
somebody else's enjoyment. I can't die because I am held in place by a powerful
bind that I can't break. Life I unfair in that way. Life is a monster. I am a monster.
I just want to die sometimes, bit I can't. I have to live for her now. She needs me.
I can't be selfish with her around.

I talk about people lying to one another. About people forgetting their
mistakes. About people not accepting people or that natural, but it all boils down
to the image of the self. We spend our lives creating what we want to be. Our parents build us up from the ground up, and then by the time that we can actually start
to make our own minds up, we are still prisoners to what we were built upon. Our
foundations of our lives are everything to a person. Without a steady foundation,
then we are nothing, and nobody wants to be nothing. Our image of our selves is
our greatest downfall in life. We are all not worth living. We are all garbage people,
but we are all humans. We make mistakes. We make up lies. We all hold in our re-
grets, because we fear what other people will think and judge us for if they find
out about our faults. We strive for perfection. We strive to be better than our parents. Then our own idols. Then our own friends. We want to be better. Just as that
sack-of-a-saying on how "Life is worth the experience of living each day better
than the last." Live fast. Live perfect. Live right. That is what we strive for, but
that is gone for most of us. Only a few people in this world will ever know how to
truly live, and it is with them that we should strive to live for.

Life is unfair. It is faulty, but it is not unpractical. It has a message for
each and every one of us. What each of those messages are, though, that is up for
debate, I guess.

I took my focus from the fire and looked at Claire. Her life is still beginning. She has the will to change and be better than us all. She can be the one to
save us, or to doom us all. That is the excitement of having a child. It is about the
possibility that they could help to save the world, make a difference, or to help to
end the world and to cause destruction. We love our children no matter what, but
we want them to help the world. We want them to strive high, to hit high, and to
stay up there in the clouds. We want them to be dreamers, not corruptors. I pity

the children of the world. They have stress placed upon them more so than my generation did. We were told that we were the ones that had to save the world. It was our responsibility, but we failed. Now, the new generation is placed with the same task, but with more stress and focus placed upon them. I pity the children of this world.

Yet, with Claire, I saw somebody different. She could be anything that she wanted to strive for. Life was her only challenge in this world. There are no social structures. There are no set religions. There are no set governments. There are no set genders. The world is full of blankness now. It has been this way for over three hundred years. I was told that I am like my great, great, great grandfather. He started our family on this path of thinking. When I first heard of his ideas, I thought that he was a genius, but when I grew up and I actually thought about these ideas, I realized that he was an idiot and a fool. However, when my mother gave me all of his journals that he wrote in, all the books that he wrote, and all the books that he read (my mother was a hoarder), I began to see his way of thinking. I appreciated him again as a person, and I realized that he was possibly the last smartest person in the world.

I sighed. So much has changed since then. I can't believe what has happened within my own lifetime.

"Are your hurt?" I heard Claire ask.

I looked up to her.

"Do you mean my wound?" I asked.

She nodded.

"I am fine. I bandaged it up when we set up camp. It should be fine in a few days." I answered her.

She smiled at me. "Good! I'm glad that you are okay. I was afraid whenever I saw that creature bite you and I heard you scream. I was so afraid." She started to shake.

I got up from my seat and wet over to her. I started to hug her.

This is why I do this. She worries about me. I need this just as much as she needs this.

I held onto her. She stopped shaking and hugged me back. She is still just a kid. She needs to know that somebody is here for her whenever she needs somebody.

Eventually, I let go of her and I returned to my seat. I put some more wood into the fire to keep us warm throughout the night. I laid myself down on the ground, and as I closed my eyes, I heard the familiar sound of shuffling towards me. I felt Claire lay down close by me. I smiled.

This felt good.

"Good night, Eilif." I heard Claire say to me.

"Yeah, good night." I said back to her.

I closed my eyes. I felt better. That is the strangeness of life. One moment you are all angry and ready to tear somebody apart and the next you are feeling so serene and safe. I don't know what more to say.

"I hope that you are watching, old man. I don't plan on giving up this journey." I thought to myself before drifting off to sleep.

Fin.

# 11.

## Open-up to Rose Tower Part 1

The morning's light had woken me up. I opened my eyes and saw that the sun was just reaching us. The fire was all burnt out- only the ashes remained from the fire of last night. I moved a little just to get some feeling into my body. I hate when I sleep wrong, and I feel stiff the next morning.

I stood up and looked at Claire. She was still sleeping. I went to my bag and decided to do what I have been doing the last few mornings. Grabbing more wood. Making a new fire. Grabbing some food. Making the food. Wrestling with my thoughts, and eventually Claire will wake up.

It is the same thing. I felt that I should hate this type of life- the familiarity, I mean- but I don't. My entire life has been built on following a schedule of the day. Sure, I got bored here and there, but I never changed my day to anything extreme. Doing something the same everyday creates a structure that prepares you for your day. The great philosophers of my time told everybody this. Well, they are all dead now. Thank God for that.

Well, I did what I always do. I grabbed the wood. I built the fire. I grabbed some food to cook, and I cooked it while thinking. Today, it was all about schedules. Damn! How bored can a person get out here? I have always been prone to do the same thing, but with Claire here it makes everything seem different. At first, it was all about me. Now, it was all about us. Survival for the both of us. Live life as a unit or die as a unit (some more crappy piece of ancient wisdom).

Yet, I still stand by what I said. I have always tried to keep a structure. It makes me feel that my day is going somewhere. It makes me feel that I can make good choices in life- at least, for the small choices.

As I was thinking about this, I saw that Claire was already standing up. She came over to me and sat down on the rock across from me. I looked at her. It still amazed me how she looked so happy in the mornings. I never understood that about children. They were happy waking up in the morning when they had no concept of what was in store for them. Old people woke up because they understood two things: (1), they are going to crock at any moment now, and (2), that if they don't get up early and start on any task that they need to do, then it may never get done tomorrow. For them, it is about death and the fear of becoming crippled. I didn't feel sorry for them, though. Humans are all fucked up and a corruptible breed. We live life to crush others only to get what we want. Well, that is a small part of the puzzle anyway.

"How did you sleep?" I asked Claire.

She looked at me and smiled. "Good."

I nodded at that. "Here, have some breakfast. We are going to be traveling a great deal today." I told her.

"Where are we heading?" she asked me.

"We are heading west. If we are lucky, we will arrive at the nearest town by nighttime, but that is only if we leave in ten minutes. You eat, and I will pack up everything."

"Okay."

I started to pack up everything lying around. Meanwhile, Claire spent her time eating her food. I kicked out the fire even while it was still ablaze, but I didn't care. I needed some heat in my step this morning.

After Claire finished eating, we set off on our journey. The leaves on this side of the bridge were a mix of orange, red, and yellow. I saw that the sun had just passed over the mountain tops and was now shining down upon us. Shit! I hate the sun. It makes me feel slow.

TIME SKIPS ON

As I was walking, I kept watch on our surroundings. People never walked on these paths or roads anymore. They stayed where they were born. Some were lucky enough to travel outside their birthplaces to other towns or cities for business or leisure. However, everybody mainly stayed where they were born because they had no interest in leaving their homes. The outside world represented oppression to them. Since the fall of the Kingdom, they have feared the outside world. There were bandits. There were legendary beasts. There were gangs. There could be as little as two or as long as five thousand miles in between one civilization and the next. Cars were a luxury item. People of high stature had cars. For everybody else, they had to walk.

People, also, didn't leave their homes because they didn't trust other people outside of their own cultures. Of their own languages. Of their own identities. Of their own appearances. It was a world that turned itself inside out. There was no point in knowing other people because they were content with their lives. So, why would they try harder in life to know somebody else? It was all about what was comfortable and what was easy. That's another reason that I hated people. They are all too simple and selfish.

As a result, these roads were all abandoned for people to walk on with nobody to ruin you. The road represented a time of freedom. If you wanted to know yourself or if you wanted to get away from life, then you could just pack up your things and walk on the road and never look back. That is what freedom is in this time. It has nothing to do with thinking. With loving. With appreciating life. With accepting each other. Freedom now is about getting away from the world. Getting away from all the bullshit. From what pisses you off.

I understand that.

Anyway, we kept walking. Nothing was happening. It felt like the old days before I took Claire along with me. It was me, and that was great. However, I felt better when she was around. She made my life mean something more than it already does. I felt better about myself (if only for a short time).

"What are you thinking about?" I heard Claire ask me.

"Uh! Oh, nothing. I was just thinking about the birds." I lied to her.

"What about the birds?" she asked.

I thought for a moment before I decided to speak.

"They are the most free out of every living animal in life." I said.

"What do you mean?" she asked me.

"They can fly. They go places. They move one way during the warmer months and elsewhere during the cold months. They create homes wherever they want to. They raise themselves as they want to. They fly. They protect. They nurture. They live, and they crap on people and their belongings, which is funny to me." I told Claire.

She smiled. "I like that."

"Do you like birds?" I asked her.

She looked up into the sky. "I never really thought about birds before. They were just there. They were just a part of life that I never noticed their lives." She started. "Yet, I have always found them more beautiful than any animal that I know. I have only seen a few before, but my favorite is a blue bird."

I listened to her. It amazes me how we change so fast. Children grow up so fast that they don't pay attention to what is going on around them. When they finally reach that age where they begin to act curious about everything that interests them, the world really opens-up for them. However, they then go through a second stage that is similar to their toddler years, and when that happens, their interests begin to focus. Yet, it is not until their late teen years and early twenties that they settle down for life on what they may what of it. We spend our whole lives shortening up our interests, but we never fully watch when life passes us by. However, we learn too late about it, and by then, we have already skipped the memories of our early years.

That is when we mourn for them. That is when we say to ourselves, "I wish that I was younger." We don't want to be young again for the memories. We hated ourselves when we were all young. No, we want to be young again to re-experience everything that they overlooked in their lives. A tree. A cloudy day. A specific toy. Something that belonged to us or that we lived through, but that we have forgotten because it was not important then.

In short, we never understood the idea of time and what it takes from us. Time is not prejudiced. Time has no hatred for a specific group. It only works as it has only worked. It steals what we do not carefully watch. I pity people. I pity the world. I pity the pitiless.

Anyhow, we kept walking. I kept watch around us for any activity of bandits. I heard nothing. I didn't feel anything, either. Everything was quiet and calm. I knew that this would not last for long. I sighed. Life tears any peace that a person may get the moment that said person realizes that they are in a peaceful situation.

TIMES PASSES ON AND ON

We have been walking for a long time now. We stopped twice for a break. Claire needed to rest for a while. She is still not used to walking this much. However, we were soon back on our path.

"What town are we going to?" she asked me.

I looked at her and then back at the road. "We are heading to Rontar Pitter town. It is one of five large towns on our way to Yondaster. It is a wealthy town known for its manufacturing of robotic body parts and system analyzers for modern cars. It is better than the last place that we were at." I told her.

"Is it a beautiful town?" she asked me.

I thought for a moment. It had been a while for me since I was last there.

"Yeah. It has modern living, transporting homes, and thirty second food stores." I told her. "There is even a park there. The grass is all natural, but the trees are fake. They also have a zoo there to. If I remember correctly."

She screamed in joy. "A zoo! I love zoos. Can we visit there? Please, Eilif?" she begged me.

I looked down and she was giving me the "puppy dog eyes". I sighed. "Sure." I finally said to Claire.

She ran to me and hugged me. I just stood there. I didn't hug her back, but instead I placed my hand on her head and rubbed her hair.

We kept walking. The weather was still good.

Suddenly, I felt that we weren't alone. I looked forward and I saw a man running towards us. I stopped and grabbed Claire by her arm and pulled her behind me. As the man ran towards us, I could see twitching in his eyes. He wasn't crazy. He looked scared of something.

As he was running by us, I reached out my arm and he ran into it and fell over. He fell back on the ground.

I looked down at him. He was a weak-looking man who had on a black suit, sandals, and a straw hat. He looked weird.

I grabbed him and picked him up before I spoke to him.

"What is going on here? Are you insane or are you scared shirtless?" I asked him.

He was shaking. I saw his eyes twitch. He looked like a noob. He was so weird that I wanted to put him out of his misery, but Claire was here.

He looked at me.

"I..."

"Yes?" I asked him.

"I am leaving Rontar Pitter." He finally said.

"That doesn't sound good." I thought to myself. I sighed. Just another issue that I need to take care of.

'Why are you leaving Rontar Pitter?" I asked him.

"Because... the people... they are all... dead." He said to me.

At this, I couldn't help but to open my eyes wide. Last that I heard, this town had well over twenty thousand people living in it. What could have happened that killed everybody there.

He started to shake again. With this, I held onto both of his arms to keep him from falling down. "That is impossible! There are too many people there for all of them to just die at once. What happened to them? A plague? An earthquake? A beast?" I asked him.

He looked at me with wild eyes. "It wasn't anything natural. It was one person that killed them." He said to me.

"What? One person?" I whispered.

He shook his head. I let him go and he ran away. I looked straight ahead. "There is no way one man could have killed everybody except... No! It is not him! I have to stop myself from thinking of that. He is gone!" I thought to myself.

It was at that point that I felt a hand slipping into mine. It was Claire. She looked up at me. I looked down at her. She looked worried, but I couldn't say anything. I just kept staring straight ahead of me. I looked into the blank and endless road.

"Eilif? Are you okay?" she asked me.

"Yeah." I answered her after a few moments. I still couldn't believe that a whole town was gone. There is no way that what that man said it right.

"Are we still going to Rontar Pitter?" she asked me.

I looked down to her.

"Yes, we are. I want to see if what that man said is true. If it isn't, then we have a place to stay for the next few days, but if he is right, then I know another place that we could go to instead. Okay?"

"Okay." She said.

I sighed. I started to walk again, and Claire followed me.

TIME PASSES: THE TOWN OF DESTRCUTION

We traveled around three more miles until we reached the opening of the town. I kept walking, not stopping for a moment until I saw for myself what was happening. As I walked through the streets, I noticed that everything was silent.

I was walking around, but I did not see anybody. The whole place looked abandoned. It almost seemed that everybody left on their own, but I didn't feel that was the answer. I smelled something in the air. It was blood. Fresh blood!

I was now running to the center of the town. When I arrived there, I was shocked beyond belief. Everybody within the whole town was in a huge pile in the center of the town. I saw whole bodies. I saw pieces of arms, legs, and heads all piled in the huge hill. Blood soaked the area. It was a pool of death with two feet worth of blood. I fell down on my knees. I just stared in horror at the scene before me.

It was a mountain of human parts. Some whole. Some just pieces. It was just utter paralyzing.

I heard somebody behind me. I saw Claire. Her face spoke a thousand fears. A thousand worries. A thousand horrors. I saw her, but she was just frozen. She could not move. I don't blame her. To see this… I was just as shocked as her.

I looked down and I could see my reflection within the pool of blood. I saw IT staring at me. I looked at IT, and I just stared. I didn't feel the need to yell. The need to tell IT to leave. I just stared at IT, and IT stared back at me. I saw the same look in IT's eyes. It thought the same as me, but I still couldn't come to the real truth that it was him. I just couldn't believe that he was alive.

I finally stood up. I started to walk closer to the bodies. They smelled like tar mixed with oil and dunked in pig feces. That is how the smell was to me. My mind was so focused on the scene before me that my stomach didn't care about the smell. I have seen many things in my life, but this brings horror to me- not because of the mountain of dead bodies, but because of how similar it is. It is the same thing that occurred twenty years ago. I could still remember that day. It is forever stained within my mind.

Everything was just still. The town was still. The bodies were still. The air was still. Nothing seemed to move. Nothing wanted to move. It was as if life said that today was a day of unmovingness.

I sighed. That is all that I could do. I just sighed. This is what life has in store for me. This is what I am used to seeing. This is what I am used to seeing within my dreams every damn night. I sighed. Life is something.

I turned around and headed back to Claire. When I reached her, she was still standing still. Frozen. I bent down to her height and looked at her face. Those once amber eyes that were full of life were now full of shock, fear, and tears. I understood that feeling all too well.

"Claire?" I whispered to her.

She didn't move. I tried again.

"Claire. Can you move?" I asked her.

She shook her head. I sighed. I stood up and grabbed her. I held her just like a person would hold their bride. I carried her away from this mess. I looked down at her. She was still in shock. Her eyes were still open. However, I saw her sink her head into my chest and start to cry and scream out loud. She was breaking inside, I knew that. I sighed. Life takes what it wants, and all we can do is bend down and take the treatment before us. I sighed

TIME SKIP

I walked with Claire in my eyes, and together I took us out of Rontar Pitter. I went through the town until I reached a large tower. This was an old lookout tower back during the time of the last war (at least forty years ago). It has since been used as a place for storage. Nobody lived here but an old lady. She was the last of a long line of people in charge of the tower. It was her history. It was her child.

I walked up to the tower. Compared to other towers out there, this one was rather larger. It was roughly two hundred feet high or so.

I walked up to the door, and I knocked on it. I didn't expect an answer after what I saw, but the old bag always told me to knock. She hated when I just let myself in. It was rude to her.

I waited and waited. I started to get impatient. I opened the door myself and walked in.

Compared to other watch towers, this one has a spacious bottom. It has a couch, a kitchen, a bathroom, a living space, and a closet. (Actually, on each floor of this place, there is a similar setup. As well as ten floors, there is a large floor that is used for nothing but storage and documentation). I looked around. It looked like nobody has been here for a while. I went over to the couch and sat Claire on it. I placed my coat over her.

After I did this, I walked over to the kitchen area.

"The old bag always has some water in the fridge." I thought to myself.

I went over to the fridge and opened it. Nothing was in it. Damn! Why is it that I can't ever get what I want? I sighed. I went over to the bathroom. I went inside and closed the door.

I turned on the facet and splashed water in my face. I looked into the mirror, and I saw IT staring back at me.

"What do you want?" I asked IT.

"*What do you plan to do?*" IT asked me.

86

"What do you mean? I can't do anything now. The people are all dead. This is the only place that we can stay at for a while." I told IT.

"*I mean, what are you going to do about HIM?*" It asked me.

I clenched the side of the sink. Breaking it in some places. "I don't know. I see it, but I can't believe it. He was dead. He IS dead, but this is HIS work." I said to IT.

IT just stared at me. I didn't want to talk about this. I still didn't want to except this. I sighed.

"*Something has to get done.*" IT finally said to me.

I looked at IT. "I know, but I need to get Claire home before I go and try to do something about HIM. You remember what happened last time. We nearly died! If it wasn't for Starchain, we would have died!" I yelled at IT.

"*I remember, but you need to think of what to do. This is a problem. HE has HIM, and they are too much for us.*" IT said to me.

At this point, I broke the while sink in two. I didn't want to discuss this right now. I have other issues that I need to take care of.

"Leave me alone. I need to think." I said to IT as I gritted my teeth. With that, IT Left me. I was alone again.

I sighed. I didn't know what to do. I left the bathroom. As I did, I saw somebody by Claire. I ran over to that person, and before I knew it, I was thrown back by a blow from that person's hand.

"An air attack, but that can only mean." I thought as I looked up. Standing over me was the old bag. The Titan of Rontar Pitter. The Queen of the Caladriuses. Gloria the Titan.

"What did I tell you about waiting for me to answer the door? I said that if you ever entered my home again without my permission, I would hit you with an air fist." She said to me in a light-hearted tone. I saw her smile as she stared at me.

I grinned. "The same old Gloria." I thought to myself.

I got up and looked at her. She was older, but fairly the same. She wore a black flannel over a white shirt. I looked down and saw that she was wearing the same red skirt that she always wore. No matter sun, rain, snow, or hail. She wore that red skirt everywhere. Gloria was wearing her glasses on her nose. Her hair was a dark grey with a hint of brown left in it. She was shorter than me, but that didn't matter for what she is capable of.

I looked at her. She looked healthy. I was glad.

"Well, if you ever open your door when a person knocks, then I wouldn't have to come in myself." I told her.

She glared at me with an angry face before softening and holding a smile on her face. "Still the same old Eilif." She turned around and started to walk back over to the couch where Claire was sleeping. "Nice to see that you have company. How have you been?"

I sat down in a chair by her. I sighed. "It could be better."

"Who is the girl?" she asked me with a raised eyebrow.

"That is a long story." I told her.

"I have all the time in the world here, and by the way things look, you have some time on your hands to tell me about it." She said proudly.

I sighed. "Fine, but let's go to your room. I don't want Claire hearing any of this."

She nodded. "Of course."

I got up and began to walk up the stairs. As I did, I looked down to see that a fire was started downstairs in the living space.

"I'm glad that she is being so nice." I thought.

Fin.

# 12.
## Open-up to Rose Tower Part II

"So that is all of it." I finished my story of how I met Claire, how I figured what her father really wanted to do in sending her out here, how I agreed to take her home despite myself, how she was captured and I had to save her, how we have been traveling, and how we ended up here (I left out the details of Roan, the fight with IT, the fight with the Pixiu, Me killing it, and about HIM).

She looked at me. I could see that she was thinking. I wish that I could read minds (even if I could, though, Gloria's mind would probably be full of wicked and sinister thoughts).

I saw that her face turned from thinking to a smile and then to a frown.

"How is the girl?" she asked.

"I think that she is handling traveling with me fine. I mean, this is not what you would think if you were in her shoes. Your father sending you away to find your mother without a person to escort you there." I said to Gloria.

"Yes. How is that going?"

"She seems to be comfortable around me." I said.

"I am not surprised. You came to her in the lowest of her moments and showed her the honest form of human kindness. This girl is craving affection. She is hurting, and just as a wound needs a band aid to keep out the nasty parts of life, you are the person who is currently protecting her from the world. You are the one person that she can find joy and happiness with. Without you, she would be broken and confused in this world." Gloria told me.

I listened to her. I thought of some of these things before, but to hear them from somebody else, it just sounds unreal. Somebody looking up to me of all people. Of course, we tend to trust people when they don't tell you all the terrible shit and pathetic things that they have been through. Trust is not a one-way street; it is a highway. People's ideas are flowing by so fast that we can only pick up on a few details, and it is from those that we judge people on being either good, decent, or outright terrible people.

I regretted taking her in, but I couldn't just leave her. She needed to be helped, and I am prone to help people. Problem meets a possible solution, I guess.

I sighed. I looked into the fire that was going in Gloria's room. She has the best room of the place. It has a living space with a television. It has a full five-piece kitchen with a fridge, a pantry, two ovens, plenty of counter space, an island, and a separate ice box. Her room has a large bathroom with a shower and a bathtub, two sinks, a separate toilet, and two closets in it. Her own room, I do not know anything about. She never let me in there. She also has her own library and computer room. She is all high tech.

I glanced around and still my face fell into the fire. I could only stare at it. I felt that it would give me a solution to my issues, but it only showed me nothing. I sighed again.

"What is the matter? You look like you had all that natural energy of yours knocked out?" she asked me.

I stood up and I walked over to the window. I stared out and saw that it was beginning to rain. That is great! Let the blood mix with the water and flow throughout the whole town and stain the streets red with it. Let the world remember what happened here for all eternity.

I looked into the rain and saw fog. It was covering up the mountain of bodies in the street. I sighed.

"What happened here, Gloria?" I asked her.

I turned around and saw that she was staring at me. "It happened all at once. The day started out so normal. Everybody awoke and went about their day as if nothing new was going to happen. I was up top, just watching over the town. I saw somebody come from the distance. The person was wearing nothing but black. I couldn't make out the face. I looked over to the front of the town and then back to where the stranger was, but they were gone."

She stopped before continuing. "I tried searching for where they went when I heard a loud scream. I aimed my sights on where that scream came from.

I saw people lying on the ground with red coming from them. I watched as one by one people were killed and slain before my eyes. It took less than five minutes before everybody was dead. I looked and all I saw was blood and bodies. I couldn't move. It was paralyzing for me. These were all people that I knew for years and years, and now they were all gone."

She stopped and I saw a tear coming from her cheek. I handed her a tissue from the table before us. She looked at me in shock before taking it. She blew into it.

"Go on when you are ready." I told her.

She nodded at me before continuing. "As I was frozen there, I heard a loud knock on the door to the tower, but I didn't move. I heard nothing more. As you know, this tower has my families' protective spells to it (as well as some of my own designs to keep out people that I don't want to come in). I went back to look through the tower's telescope, and I saw the man in black look up at me through the telescope. I saw that he grinned at me. He then vanished. I fell back into my seat, and I started to cry after that. I didn't notice that he moved the bodies until I looked through the tower around an hour later, but he was gone. Only the mountain of people remained out there." She finished her story.

I nodded at her. She saw everything that happened, and she alone survived. That is something.

"Did you recognize the man?" I asked her.

She looked at me. She shook her head. I sighed.

"He was wearing all black," she began, "but I could tell that he had a rather large arm. It looked like a beast arm, possibly, but that is impossible."

At that I looked at her in shock. It can't be. Why can't I tell myself that with everything that has been happening that HE is back? It just shouldn't be real. It can't be real, but it is.

I sat down in the chair. I stared at the fire. It was just burning as if nothing is wrong with it. Life continues while others are gone. That is the story. That is what we live in.

I saw Gloria look at me. I looked at her. She was smiling, but in a confused way.

"You have changed so much." She said to me.

"What are you saying now, you old bag?" I asked her

"You have changed. You are no longer so angry with the world as much as you were three years ago." She started to laugh a little in an amused way. "I never thought that I would live to see the day that the great leader of the Hell core would change so much." She laughed some more.

I looked at her with a death stare, but she kept laughing. She- just like Roan- knew how to test my nerves.

"Will you just shut up! I don't give a damn about that! I have some serious shit that I need to deal with before the year is over, so I am trying to think of it all." I told her.

She looked at me and smiled. "When did it happen?" she asked.

"When did what happen?" I asked her in a half-pissed off voice.

"When did you change so much? You were so angry with the world. You hated everybody. Now, though, you are so gentle. You care for people (I always knew that), but you just seem so different now. What happened that changed you so much? Was it Claire? Was it Roan?" she asked me.

My mind froze when she mentioned Roan. I lost all train of thought.

"Damn! Why did she say that name? Why did she have to say that fucking name?" I screamed to myself.

I started to clench up. I was shaking. I stood up and went over to the window. I opened it and breathed in the wet air. I breathed in and out. I breathed in and out. I needed to calm down. I can't be losing my shit over this. I have things to do. I need to help Claire. So, suck it up!

I closed the window after a minute and looked at Gloria. She looked at me in a confused way.

"What was that for? You started to freak out when I mentioned Claire and Roa..." she stopped herself.

She looked at me. She walked up to me and looked into my eyes. She just kept looking into them before gasping and holding her mouth closed.

"Is she..." she asked.

I nodded. She just hugged me. I was just frozen. I couldn't think or do anything. I was just frozen in place.

"When? What happened?" she asked.

I told her all about it. I told her every detail. It hurt so much, but I needed somebody to know. Claire was unconscious then, so she did not remember anything that happened after I rescued her.

Gloria listened to me. As she did, I saw tears roll down her face.

When I finished, everything was silent. There was no noise except for the fire. I stared at it. I couldn't stop staring after it. Fire was life. It was the creation of something else that kept burning form that life. I sighed.

I didn't tell her about who killed her, though. I didn't want her to worry about HIM. Instead, I told her that Roan didn't have time to tell me about who attacked her before she died. I never wanted life to end like this.

"Is that why you have changed so much?" she asked me.

I didn't answer her.

"I only know a few people who know anything about you besides myself. We all consider you an equal friend, but you are so mysterious. You don't ever let people in, but Roan was that one exception. She let herself in and you paid the price for that."

I didn't say anything. I didn't want to say anything anymore.

"This girl has been through so much, and here you are trying to help her to get home despite what you think of her father. You went to rescue her and, as a result, Roan died. She left you here to suffer. How does a person function? You are in so much pain each time that I see you, but this girl has obviously brought some light into your life. She has been helping to heal you as much as you have been helping her to trust and heal as well."

I looked at her. I just looked at her. She was the master of the healing powers. Her family were healers and could read the emotions of people in a way that no other people could. It also helped that she is the Queen of the Caladriuses. Those birds are healing birds. They take in the sickness of people, hold it in, and heal themselves as they heal the other person at the same time. She was that type of person. She understood suffering.

"I miss her." I said after a while. "I miss her so much that it hurts." I said to Gloria.

She placed a hand on my shoulder. I looked at her.

"We all lose people. I just lost everybody in this once peaceful town. You are not alone in that suffering." She said to me.

I nodded at her.

Silence. That was all that occurred. Pure, unbreaking silence. It was deafening. I didn't know what to say to Gloria. I didn't know what to say anymore. I sighed.

I stood up and walked closer to the fire. I needed to focus on Claire. We need rest and more supplies for food. Maggie only gave us some medical supplies to last for four months. We needed food. We needed transportation. We needed rest.

I looked over to Gloria.

"Do you think that we can stay here for the night before we leave? Claire needs to rest and calm her mind. I need to restock on supplies while we are here, too." I asked Gloria.

She nodded. "Of course, you can stay. I want to get to know this girl that you are helping so much."

"That is fine with me. Just try not to fill her head with those crazy ideas of yours." I told Gloria.

"Hey, they aren't crazy. They are innovative. Just you watch, I will turn the world around with my fancy ideas. That is if I can find the time to write them down." She said to me.

I grinned. She never did have the most organized mind, but she was clever.

I walked over to the kitchen and grabbed some water out of it.

"Hey, did I give you permission to take that?" she asked me.

I grinned at her. "No, but I am thirsty. See ya." I said before making it to the door and out before she could do anything to me.

"I will get you for that later!" she screamed as I was walking downstairs.

I laughed to myself. I felt better after that.

I walked downstairs and into the living space where I left Claire. She was still sleeping. I sighed.

I walked over to her and placed that water by her on the table. I looked at how peaceful she looked when she slept. I sighed.

I turned around and looked at the chair. I went over and sat down. I closed my eyes, and I drifted within myself to dream. I just wanted to let this day fly by and become the past. I just wanted to see a brighter tomorrow. I needed a better tomorrow, I guess.

Fin

To be continued in book II